DOMINIQUE DAOUST

Hollywoodland Magic

The Silver Screen Coven Series – Book 1

First edition

ISBN: 9798215200759

This book was professionally typeset on Reedsy.
Find out more at reedsy.com

Chapter 1

Spring 1932

Annabelle took a deep breath and opened the door to join the meeting where they were already up in arms about a potential scandal to squash.

"His devoted fans cannot find out, under any circumstances, that he has another wife out in Kansas who is twenty years his senior. We need to get her out of the picture with a divorce settlement before articles about bigamy start circulating in every Los Angeles newspaper. Now, what would you boys do to redirect the story if need be?" Nelson Beauregard, the head of MGM's publicity department noticed his new hire was hovering in the doorway. "Come in, Miss Stonewood, you're just in time to jot everything down."

Annabelle flashed her trademark smile and sat at the end of the table full of men who had not stopped talking to acknowledge her presence, cigarette smoke floating through the air like clouds. She opened her brand-new notebook, positioned her fountain pen, and started scribbling their ideas down.

"If we give her enough dough, she won't even attempt to oust him."

"We can strike first and tell the reporters there's a deranged fan going around claiming she's married to him. That way if she does come forward, she'll look like the looney one."

"We could play innocent, saying it was a simple misunderstanding and the divorce papers were lost so he thought everything was dandy."

Although she didn't know who they were talking about or what to make of it, Annabelle wrote down every single idea thrown out there. It's only once the men had exhausted their schemes for the time being that her new boss thought of making formal introductions.

"Where are my manners? Fellas, this is Miss Annabelle Stonewood, our new publicity assistant. She was an extra for a spell but we poached her. Miss Stonewood, welcome to Metro-Goldwyn-Mayer's publicity team!"

The team of a dozen men mumbled variations of the word *welcome* as they sized her up. Most of them appeared to be middle-aged, like Mr. Beauregard, but she noticed a few younger faces as well. The mention of her being an extra seemed to have piqued their interests.

"How did you become an extra, sweetheart?" one of the older men asked boldly, while lighting another cigarette. "Don't get me wrong, you have a pretty face, blonde hair, and a swell figure, but do you have connections?"

"I entered a contest back home and won a spot as an extra on Norma Shearer's last picture," Annabelle explained sweetly. She was used to such silly comments.

"I detect a slight drawl. Let's see here, are you from Kentucky?" another chimed in. "No, Missouri?"

"No, I'm from Galveston, Texas," she said proudly. "I used to do beauty pageants."

The moment the word *pageant* left her lips she regretted it. A wave of obvious snickering followed but she kept her composure. After all, it was better they heard it from her than through the grapevine.

"Say, those pageants are tough! My sister does a lot of them back in New Jersey," one of the younger fellas chimed in. "I'm Cooper Mason, by the way."

"Thank you, Mr. Mason." Now Annabelle's smile was somewhat genuine. "I do believe those skills will translate well to this department where appearances and reputations are a top priority. It's all about adapting to expectations."

"Very well said, Miss Stonewood." Nelson Beauregard nodded eagerly. "Plus, the female stars can get a little squeamish if a man tries to handle a delicate situation, so having a woman on board makes it easier. Like Louis B. Mayer always says, MGM is a big family and we need to take care of each other. All those big marquee names sign detailed contracts and despite their best efforts, sometimes an unsavory story rears its ugly head. And that's where we come in to smooth things over and make sure our studio's reputation is intact. We're one of the top studios in town for a reason!"

"We don't want no sensationalistic performers like that stage dame Mae West—what a floozy!" one of the older gentlemen chimed in, getting roars of laughter in response.

Annabelle bit her tongue and kept quiet, it wasn't the time or place to announce she was a fan of West. "So, what would you like me to do?"

"Well, it will really depend on the day and what we need."

3

Mr. Beauregard thrummed his fingers on the desk. "Usually there's a lot of typewriting, mail to be handled, and memos to be fetched. This is an extremely fast-paced environment and you need to be on your toes! We're about to take a little break from our meeting, so how about you take our lunch order and go place it with the canteen? Since you were an extra for a few weeks, you're somewhat familiar with the lot, correct?"

"Yes, a little." Annabelle flipped her notebook to a new page. "What will your orders be?"

The group barked their elaborate orders at her and all she could think was *Wow, the canteen can make all of this for them?* Granted, the publicity department was regarded in much higher esteem than a lowly extra, so it made sense that the cooks would bend over backward for them. She couldn't dare imagine what Greta Garbo or Wallace Beery ordered! But her mouth salivated at the thought of spotting some Southern barbecue dishes there one day.

"Now if you get this right, we could promote you to some more important tasks." Her boss winked at her.

"All right, I'll hold you to it!" Annabelle stood up and pointed a playful finger at him. "I'll go place your orders right now."

"Do you know who Joan Crawford is feuding with now?" an older man asked the group as Annabelle started closing the door behind her.

"You mean besides Norma Shearer, the First Lady of the lot?" a younger one responded.

"Her former co-star, Anita Page! And let me tell you it's a doozy ..."

Annabelle took a moment to lean on the door, letting out a deep sigh before slithering her way through the building and

4

stepping outside. She squinted against the bright sun and hopped on a nearby trolley that would take her all the way to the canteen. These trolleys were for the average employees who needed to get around quickly, but the stars often used their own private vehicles with chauffeurs for some privacy.

It was her first day as a member of the publicity department and she couldn't help feeling both excited and disappointed. She thought all those beauty pageant trophies would amount to something in the business, but it turns out you need to be more than a young, pretty face to make it big. Granted, her short stint as an extra taught her many tricks of the trade that she would value forever but she certainly didn't expect to pivot into publicity. But she meant what she said back there; she had a keen eye for details and her lifelong skills at creating an ideal appearance and reputation would be high currency amongst those men. They could only glean so much beyond their own egos after all.

The trolley stopped in front of the MGM canteen and Annabelle hopped off, peering down at the extensive lunch order.

"Those cooks better hold on to their spatulas because this is one long, eclectic order!" she mumbled as she made her way through a sea of hungry Metro-Goldwyn-Mayer employees eagerly starting their lunch breaks.

Chapter 2

Slightly frazzled with a delivery boy in tow, Annabelle barely had time to plop the lunches down on the table before the hungry publicity men lunged forward and devoured them like a bunch of chimpanzees. Wanting a moment to breathe, she headed out the back door to eat her tomato sandwich in peace. But she barely had a whole twenty minutes to herself before Nelson beckoned her back inside.

"We have a task for you, Miss Stonewood," he said, shoving a cigarette in his mouth as he was still chewing his lunch. "There are some members of the press who'll be here any minute. They want to walk around the lot to get a behind-the-scenes look at MGM, but no exclusive interviews with the stars or anything like that. Now, these reporters aren't exactly the cream of the crop; I wouldn't assign you to this task if it were the *Los Angeles Times* or the *Hollywood Reporter*! These are newsies from *Photoplay, Modern Screen* and the like. I want you to escort them around, try to answer their questions diplomatically, and redirect them if they get too nosy. Are you up for it?"

"Of course, Mr. Beauregard, you can count on me!" Annabelle beamed. Not only was her people-pleasing side taking over, but she was giddy about actually having the time to roam around this gigantic movie studio lot. She could tell by her new colleagues' expressions that this wasn't a coveted task, but she didn't mind one bit. It was right up her alley.

"That's the spirit!" Nelson glanced at his watch. "You better get a move on; they should be at the front gate in fifteen minutes."

Annabelle turned on her heels, downed the Coca-Cola bottle she was holding, and made tracks. She hopped on a crowded trolley which took her all the way to the main entrance gate, where three reporters were being questioned by the security guard. To her surprise it was three women. She explained the situation to the guard who graciously let them in, each blabbering on at warp speed about who they were: Babs Holbrook from *Screenland*, Cricket Dougherty from *Modern Screen,* and Adela Rogers St. John from *Photoplay.*

"Please, ladies, one question at a time! I will answer all of them to the best of my ability." Annabelle instructed them to follow her as they started their tour amongst the hustle and bustle, needing to stay alert to dodge props and carts left and right. She had a few butterflies in her stomach and kept wiping her clammy hands on her wrap dress. After all, it was her first time acting as a spokesperson of sorts for the studio but she wasn't about to let these dames know that.

"Tell me Miss ...?" Babs asked, her hands firmly clutching her pen and notebook as her eyes took in everything around her like a hawk.

"Stonewood! Annabelle Stonewood," she blurted.

"Miss Stonewood, what are the most talked-about movies currently being filmed on the lot?" Babs asked.

"Let's see, *Grand Hotel* is in post-production and that will be a swell extravaganza. It stars the Barrymore brothers,

7

Wallace Beery, and both Greta Garbo *and* Joan Crawford. What more could you ask for!" Annabelle rattled on as they moved past a fake western town comprising a desert landscape and a rundown saloon.

"What about the filming of *Red-Headed Woman*? I hear they've cast Jean Harlow in the lead role," Cricket chimed in, ready to catch a scoop.

Annabelle took a beat before answering, scanning her brain, and remembering this information had been released to the press while she was still an extra. She had to be sharp with these reporters, she didn't have the luxury of slipping up and revealing something that was supposed to stay under wraps. "Yes, she's set to star! Chester Morris and Leila Hyams have also joined the cast plus Anita Loos is writing the screenplay. I smell another box office hit for MGM!"

The trio of fan magazine reporters flung questions at her as they walked across the entire lot, from the set resembling the streets of New York City all the way to the man-made lake and the props and costume buildings. They paused in front of a few soundstages with the red lights flashing, indicating they were filming inside and not to enter at all costs.

"So, tell me, are Clark Gable and Joan Crawford going to leave their respective spouses to marry each other? Their affair is the talk of Tinseltown," Adela asked bluntly, her sharp eyes trained on the new publicity assistant.

"Oh, applesauce! Their chemistry is absolutely magnetic on screen and I can see why people jumped to that conclusion but it's just a rumour." Annabelle shrugged, feigning innocence even though this darn affair was one of the worst kept secrets on the lot. "Would you ladies like to stop by the commissary for a soda before we head over to the fan mail department? You wouldn't believe the number of letters all the marquee names receive!"

She coaxed them forward, her hairline sweating about that bullet she just dodged. She surely wouldn't last long in the publicity department if she couldn't fib believably about the rampant number of affairs behind the scenes. They were about to enter the cool air of the canteen when two famous familiar faces bumped right into them: William Powell and Carole Lombard.

"Well, well, well, isn't it The Three Stooges?" Carole teased, always the prankster. "I'm sorry but I don't have any scoops for you today, unless you consider me eating an ice cream sundae noteworthy."

"Come along dear, we have a meeting in a few minutes," Powell nodded as he led his wife by the waist. "Excuse us, ladies."

To Annabelle's utter horror, the trio of reporters started following the famous couple, launching nosy questions at their backs.

"What's this meeting about?" Cricket asked.

"Tell us, is it about your next big picture? Can you spare any details?" Barbs cut in.

"When will you two start a family? Your fans are clamouring to know!" Adela barked, the loudest of them all.

"Now that's enough of that!" Annabelle raised her voice, to her own surprise. It was loud enough to make them all spin around, including Carole and William. "As I've told you from the start, this tour is about getting a behind-the-scenes look at the lot, not to pester the actors. Now if you don't stop harassing

9

them this instant, I will escort you back to the front gate."

"Wow, this tomato has claws," Adela smirked as she exchanged an amused look with her fellow reporters. "All right, we catch your drift. Let's go get sodas to cool off."

"Thanks kid, I owe you one." Carole winked at Annabelle before turning back around, her arm linked with her husband's as they strolled away.

Carole Lombard was in her mid-twenties, which only made her a few years older than Annabelle, but nevertheless this newbie assistant looked up to this screwball comedienne. She would love to spend an evening picking her brain about show business, but she had to put that thought aside for now.

Annabelle threw out all the fun facts she could think of to stop the trio from asking prying questions, and the rest of the tour went on without a hitch. She walked them back to the front gate and wished them a nice evening as they departed. She couldn't tell if they were impressed with her for being stern or if they were dissatisfied to leave with no juicy scoops. Regardless, Annabelle was proud of herself for holding her own with that pack of wolves.

"Jeepers, that was a lot to handle," she mumbled as she slowly shuffled back to the publicity department.

Chapter 3

Eager to receive a pat on the back for her efforts with the fan magazine trio, Annabelle was somewhat disappointed to get no such acknowledgement from her new boss. Nelson Beauregard simply gave her a stern nod and told her to show up bright and early tomorrow morning.

"I guess I was reaching for the clouds a little bit," she sighed as she exited MGM's front gates with a throng of exhausted cast and crew members.

A huge chunk of the crowd shuffled to the gigantic parking lot where their cars were stowed away, but Annabelle walked to the corner and hopped on the Red Car. Her feet throbbed uncomfortably as she stood up and held onto an overhead railing for good measure. Luckily her commute was short since she was renting out a room in an apartment building in the Fox Hills neighbourhood of Culver City.

The apartment building was gloomy even on a sunny day and Annabelle had yet to cross most of the tenants after a few months of living there. She assumed they all had nighttime odd jobs, but she really didn't know. She let herself in, grabbed a croissant and an apple from the communal ice box, and walked up the rickety stairs.

"Every damn time," Annabelle grunted, having to shove her shoulder into the door to enter her room. Thankfully the room itself looked better than the rest of the building and she even had her own private bathroom which was a must for her.

She poured herself a glass of water from the sink, sat cross-legged on her bed and nibbled on her croissant. Her eyes once again travelled to the nightstand where she snatched up the open letter lying there tauntingly. It read:

Dearest Annabelle,

We do hope you're settling into your new city nicely. Folks back here still can't believe you won that contest. From pageant queen to an MGM extra, that makes their heads spin! We sure do miss having you around but we're so proud that you're making your dreams come true.

With love,
Mother & Father

"Jeepers, this makes me both happy and sad at the same time," Annabelle blurted, tossing the letter aside as she held back tears. "They gotta stop making it look so simple in the pictures. The odds of getting discovered amongst a sea of hopefuls are nearly nonexistent!"

Back in Texas, when she joined beauty pageants all around the state, she was a recognizable face from Galveston. The more accolades she garnered, the more people wanted to be around her. But her family knew to keep her humble. After all the smiling and strutting for crowds, she'd come home to the farm and help with chores without whining or trying to find reasons to avoid them. It was a good combination which she might have taken for granted, but she couldn't stop herself from reaching for the stars.

The day that talent scout waltzed into her dressing room after her latest crowning and uttered the words "MGM contest for extras," Annabelle had stars in her eyes and knew she'd win a spot that would bring her all the way to Los Angeles. She was confident in her abilities and knew she had what it took to make it big.

To her credit she kept that energy up throughout her stint as an extra, but it was seeing all those other extras vying for the same fame and glory she so desperately wanted that gave her pause. What if she was only meant to be famous in a small town? What if she'd just be drowned out by all the starlets with similar ambitions out here on this prestigious studio lot?

Her insecurities were somewhat confirmed when she had been taken aside and told she wouldn't be picked up as an extra, but there was an opportunity for her in the publicity department. Taken aback, Annabelle accepted because she didn't want to go back to Texas empty-handed and she knew she had much more to offer. She just had to make the top executives see it.

"And now here I am, one day into my new job and feeling sorry for myself," she lay back on her bed, staring at the ceiling with the cracked paint veining all about. "The only dame in a department full of men with their own agendas. Heck, they can barely tolerate looking at me! How on earth did I end up in this role?"

She allowed herself five more minutes for her pity party then she sat back up, shoving all her insecurities to the back of her mind. She went to her dresser and snatched the notebook lying in wait for action, then she sat back down, tapping her favourite fountain pen on her chin.

"That's enough of that," Annabelle chastised herself. "I am lucky to be here, people would kill to be in my position! Just because I'm going through a rough patch right now, it doesn't mean I can't turn it around."

She opened her notebook to a blank page, closed her eyes and took a deep breath.

"I know I can help the publicity department create flattering images for its stars. I did it for myself on the beauty pageant trail and I know what to look for in others," Annabelle mumbled, her eyes still closed. "And I also know how to pivot a bad conversation toward a more savoury topic. I saved Miss Carole Lombard from a tense situation today and I can do it again. My new colleagues are bound to see my worth if I keep doing the gritty work. After all, my feminine disposition is bound to have some advantages in this racket!"

Annabelle spent the next five minutes writing ideas down, suggestions which she could wiggle into future meetings without seeming too pushy. God forbid a woman could hold her own and have original thoughts!

"There, I feel much better now." She stared at her page of notes, feeling a weight lifted off her shoulders. "I just need to take it one little step at a time, like a turtle, and results will surely follow."

Satisfied, Annabelle put her notebook aside, making a mental note to bring it to the studio with her tomorrow. She changed into her pyjamas and crawled into bed despite the early hour. Once her head hit the pillow, it didn't take long before she drifted off to sleep. A few thoughts mingled about as dreamland encroached her mind. One was that she had to write a letter to her parents detailing her encounter with William Powell and Carole Lombard—how they'd get a hoot from that story! And the second had to do with making friends in this strange showbiz-centred city. Annabelle could control her actions and the image she wanted to convey, but befriending people was a whole other ballgame. And despite the list she curated, she couldn't deny that finding a circle of people she could confide in was at the top of her list.

Chapter 4

The next morning, Annabelle's eyes shot open before her alarm could rattle her awake, the early bedtime she imposed on herself having done her a world of good. She got dressed while humming a jazz tune, selecting a demure grey pencil skirt with a dusty-rose blouse before primping her hair and applying some light makeup.

"Don't want to forget this." Annabelle snatched her trusty notebook from her bedside table and headed downstairs to the communal kitchen which was once again deserted. "I'm starting to think this lot are vampires like Bela Lugosi!"

She allotted herself ten minutes to eat the egg salad sandwich she had prepared in advance and washed it down with some bitter, hot coffee. She dabbed her mouth demurely with a napkin and raced out the door to catch the Red Car. Yesterday's ride home felt long and torturous but this morning she had to hold back from gabbing to all the exhausted-looking folks around her. Back home in Galveston, Annabelle could pretty much talk to all the friendly faces she came across. But here in Los Angeles, she got the nagging feeling everyone wanted to remain strangers, grumpy at the mere thought of small talk.

"Good morning, sir! Reporting for duty yet again." Annabelle bounded up to the security guard at MGM's front gate with its large Greek columns and handed him her badge and identification.

The man gave a cursory glance at the cards then handed them back to her with a grunt, not even bothering with a smile or eye contact.

"Have a lovely day," Annabelle cooed, not letting his mood damper hers. He pressed a button and the gated door opened. She was only two steps in when she heard a car screech to a halt behind her.

"Hello, Miss Davies! It's always a pleasure crossing paths with you." The security guard was now full of excitement.

Annabelle turned around and stared openly at none other than Marion Davies, the coveted star and well-known mistress of William Randolph Hearst, sitting behind the wheel of a cherry-red 1932 Ford automobile with fashionable sunglasses shielding her eyes from the early morning sun.

"Well, aren't you the sweetest." She tried handing over her badge but he pressed the gate button and waved her through right away.

"I hope you have a swell day on set!" the security guard exclaimed as he watched her car go through.

Marion Davies drove slowly through the gate, pausing when she noticed Annabelle off to the side. "I think that fella has a crush on me. Nice blouse." She lifted her sunglasses, gave Annabelle a wink and then drove away.

"Well, I'll be damned," Annabelle mumbled, almost feeling as starstruck as the security guard. But then she looked at her watch and snapped right out of it. "Shoot, I need to get to the publicity building!"

Once inside the building she finally started feeling less on edge about her potential tardiness, smoothing over her skirt as she made her way to the big conference room only to find it empty. Had they all stepped out for a minute? Mr. Beauregard had told her they started every day with a team meeting. She walked back out to the building lobby and made a beeline for the receptionist.

"Good morning, darlin'. Has the rest of the team stepped out already?" Annabelle asked, noting the young lady behind the desk wasn't the same one as yesterday. Maybe they rotated receptionists around the lot. "I'm Annabelle Stonewood, the new publicity assistant."

"Oh, it's nice to meet you! My name is Ginny. I was sick yesterday but I'm feeling right as rain today." The receptionist reached out and shook hands with Annabelle then lowered her voice. "Between you and me, this gang isn't big on punctuality. They tend to have a long breakfast in the canteen. As a matter of fact, here they are coming back now."

The group of men were laughing and chit-chatting as they entered the building, many of them only giving cursory glances to the ladies before continuing into the conference room. The publicity director is the only one who reluctantly stopped by the reception desk.

"Good morning, Miss Stonewood. I see you've met Miss Otter. She handles the phone and appointments." Mr. Beauregard waved a dismissive hand, as if those tasks were insignificant. "Now follow me, newbie, we have a meeting."

Annabelle gave Ginny a knowing smile as she followed her boss into the conference room where the rest of the team had made themselves at home, some even leaning back with their feet up against the large wood table at the centre of the room.

"Gentlemen." Mr. Beauregard cleared his throat as he sat at the head of the table. "What matters need to be dealt with today?"

"John Barrymore was once again seen around town absolutely blotto; the press will have a field day with it if we don't squash it fast," one of the older fellas grunted, his cigarette not leaving his mouth.

"Greta Garbo is still avoiding all interviews we schedule for her. She's one of our biggest box office draws, and she needs to play nice with reporters, it's part of her job," Cooper Mason offered with crossed arms. Annabelle noticed that he seemed to have a whole lot of confidence for a youngster like herself.

"There are rumours going around that some of our latest pictures are delayed and over budget. Maybe a press release could put the public at ease and help us remain as *the* prestige studio in their eyes. I'm sure Louis B. Mayer would appreciate that," another colleague chimed in.

Annabelle tried her best to keep up with the chaotic flow of conversation, trying to find the best moments to slip a word in, but her "perhaps we could," "what if we," or "have we considered," were swiftly drowned out by the louder male voices. Mr. Beauregard was the only one who seemed to have noticed her trying to speak, and he let out an exasperated sigh which silenced everyone.

"Miss Stonewood, while I understand you're trying to interject with good intentions, please remember your place in this department. You are here to observe, take notes, and do what we ask of you. Am I making myself clear?"

"Crystal clear," Annabelle kept a stony smile plastered across her face despite being mortified down to her toes. Sure, men had talked down to her plenty of times, especially on the beauty pageant circuit, but it always stung really bad. Her notebook filled with ideas would have to be put on the back burner for now.

"Splendid, that's what I like to hear." Nelson patted her knee as the rest of the men chuckled. It took all her willpower to prevent her from jerking away from his patronizing touch.

"Say boss, there's something Miss Stonewood can help us with today." Cooper Mason perked up, somewhat cutting the tension from the awkward chastising.

"And what's that?" Nelson cocked an eyebrow as he lit yet another cigarette.

"Isn't filming of *The Enchantress* starting today? Our leading lady is garnering a lot of attention lately and the press are stalking her like a hawk," Cooper explained. "Weren't you adamant that the scrutinizing from the reporters needs to be kept to a minimum?"

"You're right." Nelson scratched his chin in thought before snapping his fingers. "Miss Stonewood, you're now on chaperone duty! Let's get a move on and I'll explain what is expected of you. Meeting adjourned."

Mr. Beauregard leaped off his chair and swiftly exited the room, forcing Annabelle into a scramble to keep up.

Chapter 5

"Look here kid, what I'm about to tell you is private information and must not be shared with *anyone,* not even your colleagues. Do you catch my drift?" Nelson explained gruffly as he avoided the studio trolley and instead guided them through a longer and much quieter route through the lot.

"Yes, I understand." Annabelle couldn't help but feel giddy at the idea of being the only other person in her department knowing this privileged information.

"I'm assuming you've heard of Clover Halliwell, she recently signed a seven-year contract with us?" Nelson asked, still looking ahead and keeping up a hectic pace.

"Sure! She's gaining quite a bit of popularity with her roles opposite Nelson Eddy and Spencer Tracy. Her eyes are so expressive on screen," Annabelle mused.

"Wait until you see those big baby blues in person, she's box office gold!" Nelson seemed mesmerized just thinking about them. "Anyway, Miss Halliwell has gotten herself in a bit of a predicament. You see ... She has a bun in the oven and as you may know she isn't married."

"Oh, that is quite a predicament." Annabelle shook her head, feeling bad for the rising star. It takes two to tango yet it was always the women who had to make the tough decisions. "I take it she wants to keep the child and the people who know are in a tizzy about this being revealed to the public?"

"You're right on the money, Stonewood," Nelson sighed. "Having a child out of wedlock could really tank her career so the few of us who know have come up with a plan: once her latest picture is done filming, she'll go on an extended trip, somewhere remote like Alaska or Australia. She'll give birth and the baby will be taken care of for a few months while she comes back and resumes her career like nothing happened. Then she'll adopt her own child but the public won't know any better. It's the best we could come up with."

"If I may, it sounds a little far-fetched if you're one of the few who knows the whole story, but the scheme is plausible for everyone else." Annabelle nodded, knots in her stomach forming as they approached a long stretch of land with monstrous soundstages. "I appreciate you trusting me with this story."

"Yeah well, I didn't have much of a choice." Nelson scratched his head as he came to an abrupt halt and looked around, making sure no one was eavesdropping. "*The Enchantress* starts filming today and unfortunately Miss Halliwell is starting to show. The press are like vultures around her and everyone else on set doesn't have the slightest clue about her predicament. That's why I thought another woman like yourself could be a good chaperone, to make sure the cat doesn't get out of the bag."

"That's understandable. Am I even allowed on set? Surely, I'll need to explain my presence." Annabelle's hands were dripping with sweat. "Not only am I new here but I can only assume they don't want people lurking around sets if they shouldn't be there."

"Darn it! That's true." Mr. Beauregard pulled a slim notepad and pen from his breast pocket and scribbled frantically. "Here, that should do it."

"Hopefully this does the trick." Annabelle couldn't read his writing at all, it was just a bunch of nonsensical scratches, but she hoped whoever read it would understand. "Oh, one last thing ... Do we know who the father is?"

"Miss Halliwell hasn't uttered a word about him and I'd rather keep it that way. There are already too many love triangles, heck love *squares* going on around here, and I don't want to hear about another one." Nelson was growing annoyed; he had done enough talking for a while. "Now get a move on, I'm sure the cameras will start rolling any second."

With that Mr. Beauregard stomped away, leaving his new hire with a pretty hefty responsibility on her shoulders. Annabelle faced the looming soundstage and took a few steadying breaths, clutching her boss's note in her clammy hands.

"I can do this. It's about protecting Clover Halliwell's image at all costs," she mumbled as she approached the side door. "That's my one and only goal."

The light above the entrance wasn't flashing red, letting her know filming hadn't started yet. She opened it cautiously and walked inside, but she only got a few steps in, the door slamming shut behind her and an irritated assistant materializing out of nowhere.

"Who the hell are you?" He eyed her suspiciously then consulted the clipboard in his hands. "You're not allowed to be here."

"I have a note from Nelson Beauregard explaining my presence. I'm a new publicity assistant." Annabelle gave him her brightest smile as she handed him the note.

"Ugh, fine," He rolled his eyes and handed her back the note. "Miss Halliwell is to the right of the stage. Make sure you stay in the shadows once the camera starts rolling and if I hear even a peep coming from you, you'll be booted from this set."

"Understood. Thank you." Annabelle waltzed on by and followed his directions until she saw the rising star sitting on a chair alone decked out in a black silky dress with matching shawl, looking bored. "Miss Halliwell? I'm Annabelle Stonewood, a new publicity assistant sent over by Mr. Beauregard to act as your chaperone during filming."

"Oh ... *ohhhh.*" Clover Halliwell's blue eyes got bigger as she connected the dots, and her copper hair really made them sparkle. She talked in a breathy baby voice which often suited her sweet yet seductive roles."Well, I'm glad there's finally a woman in that department. I hope I can trust you to keep an eye out for me?"

"Not to worry, I got your back." Annabelle gave her a wink and the actress seemed to relax into the chair. Annabelle had had more direct contact with marquee names in the past two days in her new job than she ever did being an extra. "So, tell me about this movie, Miss Halliwell."

"Please call me Clover, we're practically the same age!" she said with a wave of her hand. "Oh, you know, it's about this woman who enchants men away from their wives with love potions. The usual romantic stuff."

"Well, they've surely created quite an idyllic atmosphere on set," Annabelle said as she looked around. One area appeared to be a boudoir with rich silks and velvets draped all around, and another appeared to be a quaint wood-panelled cottage where she assumed Clover's character brewed her potions.

"And how! Movie magic is really something, it all comes

together perfectly," Clover responded dreamily.

"All right, listen up folks," a man, presumably the director, boomed into a comically large megaphone. "We're still having trouble with the overhead lighting; it might take another half hour to fix so please bear with us."

A few groans were heard throughout the soundstage but the whole crew kept running about as usual, the extra time allowing them to fine-tune certain details.

"Unfortunately, there's a lot of waiting around," Clover sighed, making sure to drape her costume over her growing tummy. "Would you mind fetching me a glass of water? There's a water cooler over there by the extra scene props. I would go myself but, you know, I'm trying to limit my movements."

"Of course, I'll be back in a jiffy." As Annabelle weaved her way through a ridiculous number of bustling crew members, it seemed to her like fifty more had materialized in the mere moments since the director mentioned a delay. How could they truly keep track of who was allowed to be here while filming?

She made it to the water cooler propped up against the back wall, surrounded by props that would be added throughout different scenes. It still amazed her how many departments it took to create one single motion picture.

"Now where are those paper cups," Annabelle mumbled as she looked around. Maybe she had to let someone know they needed to be refilled.

Out of the corner of her eye Annabelle saw a thick red book fall off a teetering stack of other props. Without thinking twice, she walked over and reached down to grab it. She barely had a hand on it when she noticed three other dames had also reached down to pick it up. With their four hands grasping the prop book, Annabelle felt a strange current of energy, like a powerful static shock which jolted her into letting go of the book. It seemed like the others did the same and the prop clattered to the ground just as the power went out, sending the soundstage into complete darkness.

The director started speaking into his megaphone again but was brusquely cut off by a scream echoing from somewhere high above in this pitch-black space, rendering the hundreds of MGM staff and crew enclosed here speechless for the first time that day.

Chapter 6

The scream seemed to travel from high above in the dark until a thud was heard, which snatched all sounds from the air, making Annabelle feel queasy.

"Jeepers, that can't be a good sign," she whispered, clasping her hands together. By the void of silence surrounding her, she could tell all MGM employees trapped on this soundstage held the same fear in their guts.

Another painstaking minute passed until the power came back on, blinding everyone for a split second. The cast and crew looked around to try and find the source of the scream in the garish brightness that hovered over them. Annabelle craned her neck but her spot by the water cooler didn't give her a decent vantage point of the soundstage; from her estimation the scream came from the far-right corner.

"Hey boss, we have a situation over here!" one rough-looking crew member, one who presumably did a lot of heavy lifting, bellowed for the director to come look at his discovery.

Annabelle watched the now worried-looking director clear a path to the back right corner, as she had expected. Many people around her stayed put but she couldn't help herself from moving closer, tiptoeing behind the sets while remaining out of the way. There was a huddle of five men surrounding what looked like a body, limbs spread out at awkward angles. The men took an excruciating amount of time whispering before finally bending down to check for a pulse, their faces growing five shades whiter after doing so.

"Can I have everyone's attention please?" The director's voice wavered slightly in his megaphone. "There's been a serious accident and we need everyone to leave the soundstage immediately. I repeat, the whole lot of you need to leave *now.*"

A wave of MGM cast and crew clamoured to the main exit, the director not having to repeat himself. Annabelle's first instinct was to make sure Clover Halliwell was all right, but once she reached the spot where the star had quietly sat a few minutes ago, the chair was vacant.

"I guess her image isn't the top priority right this second," Annabelle quipped as she watched the remaining employees slam the soundstage door behind them. If she knew what was best for her, she would have followed suit and made tracks. But she couldn't stop herself from hanging back, once again finding a semi-secluded spot near the sets where she could observe quietly.

"Are we sure he's dead?" one man asked.

"Gee Frank, I think the fact that he no longer has a pulse removes him from the realm of the living," another blurted. "Plus look at the way he's contorted ..."

"What's his name, anyway?" the director asked, the megaphone now leaning on his hip. Annabelle couldn't tell if he was disturbed by the ordeal or annoyed that this would cause shooting delays.

"His name is, uh *was,* Chuck Thorne. He's been a lighting technician on the lot for a few years now." The man's head cocked upward. "Looks like he was trying to fix the lighting problem up there on the balcony and fell somehow. What a horrifying way to go."

There was a pause as the small group's attention, including Annabelle's, was redirected toward the soundstage balcony that circled high above around the sets. It almost gave her vertigo thinking about being that high up, but surely this now deceased fella was used to roaming up there for his job.

"The press are gonna have a field day with this one," the director groaned, rubbing a scruffy hand over his face. "Well, let's call it in boys. Someone ring studio security and tell them to call the police. We have a body on set."

The small group broke apart and that's when they noticed the sneaky blonde lurking by the sets.

"What do you think you're doing? We told everyone to scram, young lady!" One of the workers became indignant real fast. "Are you even an MGM employee?"

"I apologize for my perceived intrusion." Annabelle stepped forward, exuding confidence despite her jittery stomach. "I'm Annabelle Stonewood, the new publicity assistant here at the studio. I thought our department would be important to consult during such a delicate situation. After all, our job is to alleviate tensions with reporters. We wouldn't want stories going out saying MGM is an unsafe workplace now, would we?"

She was grateful a wave of moxie came over her because it seemed to have done the trick; the men were now thinking over what she said. They all shrugged, realizing she brought up an important point.

"Fine, I see what you're driving at." The director gave her a stern look. "Call Nelson and tell him to make the trek over here. We need to make sure not a single word about this is uttered to the press until the police get here and we figure out what to say."

"I'm on it." Annabelle gave them a nod then scurried all the way to the entrance of the soundstage where a telephone hung on the wall. She picked up the receiver and dialed the publicity department, where Ginny picked up on the first ring.

"Hi Ginny, could you transfer me to Mr. Beauregard's line please? It's an emergency."

"Sure thing, Annabelle. But I gotta warn you, he gets cranky when his lunch is interrupted," Ginny advised before patching her through.

"Why in the devil would you interrupt the one moment of peace I have during the entire day?" Nelson barked, his voice always at maximum volume. "I thought I made myself clear when I explained this task to you."

"Yes, you've made yourself very clear, but this doesn't have anything to do with Miss Halliwell. There's a bit of an emergency here on the soundstage—" Annabelle was interrupted.

"Let me clarify, Miss Stonewood, that you should only use the word *emergency* either when Louis B. Mayer is looking for me or if someone has dropped dead," Nelson huffed. "The rest of it can wait until I'm done my roast beef sandwich!"

"Well then I've used the word under the right circumstances sir," Annabelle swallowed. "Someone has dropped dead … emphasis on the word *dropped*."

Chapter 7

As if pulling off a magic trick, Nelson Beauregard burst through the soundstage mere moments after Annabelle called him with the terrible news. He was panting and frantic as he approached the small group at the rear huddled near the body.

"If this is some sort of prank, I will sue all of you!" Nelson's voice wavered as he got close enough to view the body.

"The props department are geniuses but unfortunately this is a real dead body, pal." One of the crew members patted a now pallid Nelson on the shoulder.

The head of publicity had seemingly forgotten his employee's presence at this morbid scene, but Annabelle didn't mind. The last thing she wanted was to be escorted out of there just when things were getting interesting. Now it was the three police officers' turn to burst through the soundstage door; Annabelle slunk a little farther back into the shadows of the set to remain unnoticed.

"Los Angeles Police Department reporting to a crime scene," the de facto lead officer announced, hands resting on his thick belt near his pistol. "We were notified of an MGM employee who had presumably fallen to his death?"

"Oh brother, now I'm sure the entire lot is running their

mouths about this," Nelson groaned, visible sweat glistening at his temples. For someone who was supposed to handle sticky situations, Annabelle felt her boss wasn't keeping his cool very well.

"We need someone to walk us through what happened," another officer asked, ignoring Nelson's comment as the trio stood right by the victim's feet.

The remaining crew members shrunk back, intimidated by the coppers, leaving the director in charge of giving the sordid details.

"Well, uh, there was a lighting problem which delayed the start of filming. We were trying to get that sorted when we lost power. It couldn't have been more than a few minutes, but then we heard a horrifying scream ... and a sickening thud. The lights switched back on soon after and that's when these crew members found this poor fella on the floor," the director explained. "I told everyone else to clear the soundstage immediately."

"That was a good call, you don't want people trampling through the area." One of the coppers nodded. "So, what's this fella's name? Was he already dead when you found him?"

"His name was Chuck Thorne and he'd been an MGM lighting technician for a few years now. We think he lost his balance up there while fixing the lights. And trust me, it was over the second he hit the floor." The crew member shivered.

"He must have hit the ground at the right angle," the lead officer commented grimly as he observed the body. "Was he the only one up there? Did anyone hear a commotion before he fell?"

"No sir, the scream came out of nowhere," another crew

member replied with wide eyes.

"Very well. Would you all please step aside for a moment as we investigate the body?" The officer waited for the crew to be sufficiently out of the way before crouching down above Chuck Thorne.

"What a nightmare," Nelson hissed as he approached Annabelle. "It was already a pain to deal with Miss Halliwell's *condition* but now we also have a death on set to contend with. Where were you standing when the power went out?"

"I was on the other side of the stage by the water cooler so I can't confirm or deny hearing a struggle prior to Mr. Thorne falling. It's all so tragic." Annabelle shook her head.

"My skin is crawling at the thought of all the cast and crew members talking about this tragedy beyond these walls! Once the coppers are done here, we need to make sure everyone is on the same page about this. God forbid reporters get a hold of them before we do." Nelson was spiraling more out of concern for the studio than the victim, and it made Annabelle queasy.

Another few minutes passed where the police officers searched around the body, one even climbing up to the balcony where the lights were set up, shaking the railing to confirm it was still sturdy and not the cause of Mr. Thorne's fall. They huddled together and whispered for a spell before asking the witnesses to join them.

"All right, we think we've gathered everything needed to determine this was a horrible accident," the lead officer announced, still in his authoritative stance. "We have to talk with all the cast and crew who were on the call sheet, but there's no physical signs of struggle up there or on the victim. We think he might have leaned over the railing too far and fell over. It's our main theory so far."

Annabelle looked around as everyone else seemed to agree with this consensus, wanting to move on. But something was keeping her on the fence.

"We'll call the city coroner at once to retrieve the body. Then we'll need to interview everyone present," the lead officer continued as the group started walking toward the front entrance to the soundstage.

Annabelle hung back and despite the terror coursing through her veins, she approached Chuck Thorne's body.

"You poor man," she whispered as she shakily crouched down, making sure not to touch him.

She had attended the funerals of distant relatives before, but she had never seen a dead body under these circumstances. Annabelle looked up at the lighting balcony looming high above her. It was this man's job to be up there all day but in the end it's what caused his demise. You'd think he would have known to be careful and take necessary precautions for his safety.

She was thinking about who would have to notify his friends and family when she noticed some distinct bruising around his upper arms.

"Are those ... finger marks?" Annabelle was bewildered as she stared at the purplish-blue bruises wrapping around his arms. "Those surely couldn't have been caused by the fall itself."

She got up and marched up to the group. They all turned toward her as if noticing the new publicity assistant for the first time.

"Ah, there you are Miss Stonewood. We have an important task for you—" Mr. Beauregard started but she interrupted him.

"Excuse me, officers, but did you not notice the bruise marks on the victim's upper arms? They look like finger marks." Annabelle stared at them expectantly. Maybe it was an innocent mistake and they had overlooked it.

"Yes, it'll be noted in our report," the lead officer replied dismissively before turning his attention back to Nelson.

"Doesn't that come across as a little suspicious? I certainly wouldn't rule out foul play with those markings," Annabelle continued, not letting it go.

"Miss, aren't you Mr. Beauregard's assistant? How about you leave the police work to the real officers, honey," the lead officer snarled before stepping outside in the sunlight.

"What the devil is wrong with you? Are you trying to go head-to-head with the LAPD?" Nelson admonished her as everyone else exited the soundstage, rays of light temporary blinding them as the door moved.

"I assure you I'm not trying to cause a fuss, Mr. Beauregard." Annabelle maintained her composure as she explained herself. "They just made it sound like a clear-cut accident when those bruises say otherwise! I thought it was oversight on their part but now it seems intentional."

"Look here, you're still new to this big city but everyone knows the coppers are crooked and dirty. It's been like this for over a decade now and I can't fathom it changing anytime soon," Nelson sighed. "So, if I were you, I would keep my mouth shut around them. These are not people you want as enemies, am I understood?"

"Yes," Annabelle quipped. What she hated more than any-thing else was dishonest hypocrites; they made her skin crawl.

"Now that we've put that matter behind us, I need you to shadow the officers for the rest of the day as they conduct interviews with the cast and crew who were on set." Nelson wagged a finger at her. "But I don't want you running your mouth. I need you to make sure everyone is on the same page from a publicity perspective. We don't want studio employees telling the press different accounts of the same story, which would be a mess for us to untangle. Can I trust you with this?"

"Yes, I'm your gal!" Annabelle forced a smile as she followed her boss out into the blinding sunlight.

The idea of the police not considering the whole truth of the incident was unfathomable to her, but at least she could gather more information during the interviews. After all, just because they didn't want to get their hands dirty didn't mean she didn't want to.

Chapter 8

Annabelle spent her lunch time hovering over a tomato sandwich, her stomach wanting no food whatsoever as Nelson Beauregard coached her on what to say to the cast and crew during their imminent police interrogations.

"So, it's important you make it painstakingly clear that no one can deviate from the story when talking to the press. No embellishments or 'what ifs'. If I catch wind of anything of the sort they'll get a personal scolding from me," he blabbered on, pushing a sheet of typewritten paper toward her. "Here, I got Miss Otter to type this up for you. It's the main points you need to emphasize when talking to these showbiz folks. They most likely already noticed you on set this morning, so your presence won't be odd but it's vital that you speak with confidence. You're representing the publicity department after all."

"All right, I catch your drift. I'll make them believe there will be hell to pay if they don't cooperate," Annabelle answered with her eyes still on her uneaten sandwich, hoping her appetite would be back in time for supper.

"Atta girl! You should probably head on over there, the coppers are gonna start their interrogations at 1:15 on the nose," Nelson replied. "You don't want them to blow their wigs by being late."

"Of course not," she replied as she stood up. "The last thing I want is for someone to be irritated with me. I'll report back here once it's all over and done with."

Ginny gave her an encouraging smile as she walked by the front desk and back out onto the open studio lot. The air was a tinge sombre compared to this morning; groups of people were talking in hushed whispers everywhere she looked. Sure, they could be talking about any number of rumours or gossip—her short stint as an extra opened her eyes about how fast those could spread like wildfire—but Annabelle was almost positive she knew what was on everyone's mind today.

She hopped on the MGM trolley and watched all the sets roll by as her mind spun around on itself. The esteemed police department were silly to jump at the possibility of an accident so quickly when there was glaring black and blue evidence that could prove otherwise. But this wasn't her first rodeo; she could play nice with people she didn't agree with. That Southern charm wouldn't be wasted today!

Annabelle exited the trolley and found herself once again in front of the soundstage designated to film *The Enchantress*, although this time her desire to go inside had dwindled considerably. She took a steadying breath, plastered on her pageant-ready smile, and opened the door. The police had set up chairs not far from the entrance, so when anyone came in, they came face to face with four stern-looking officers.

"Gee, it looks like you're going to interrogate me too," Annabelle chirped, not knowing where to stand.

"Well actually ..." one officer replied as he looked at his

colleagues. "We might as well, you were present after all. Have a seat."

"This will be rather short since I was on the other side of the soundstage," she started explaining as she sat in the lone chair facing the cops. "I walked across to get a cup of water for Miss Halliwell when I picked up a prop book from the ground at the same time as some other gals, then the power went out ..."

Annabelle got lost in thought for a moment. Something was struggling to come to the forefront of her mind but the officers had already determined that's all they needed out of her.

"That's good enough, Miss Stonewood, we understand you didn't see or hear anything. Please have a seat over here," the lead officer instructed as he flipped his notebook to a new page. "Mr. Beauregard aggressively insisted on having a publicity assistant present for this. Why he couldn't be here himself I don't understand, but here *you* are. Please refrain from talking until we're done with the interrogations."

"That's fine by me," she said, sitting down on her chair distinctly set apart from them. "I do have one question though. Why hold the interrogations in the exact location where the death occurred? Surely people will be upset enough as is."

"That's the point, sweetheart. It's to make them feel uneasy and potentially jog their memory," one officer sighed as the rest smirked at her. "Plus, this was the only free area where we could conduct them with no looky-loos. Any other questions you want to launch our way?"

Annabelle shook her head "no" while keeping a serene expression. Her best course of action, lousy as it was, was to keep quiet until expressly told to speak. She felt like she was at an oddly orchestrated pageant where there were no talent shows but an overwhelming number of stern glares instead.

As it turned out the interrogations were monotonous; the main thing Annabelle retained was who all the employees were and which departments they worked for. Even the police officers seemed bored as they asked the same questions over and over with nothing of value as responses. Then Annabelle had the courtesy of giving her publicity speech about how to deal with the press regarding this tragedy, over and over again.

Having come into these interrogations hoping to glean something of importance, Annabelle was sorely disappointed. No one saw anything amiss or suspicious. If anything, it just proved all employees were concerned with their specific tasks and didn't pay attention to their surroundings. Part of her understood because so much goes on while on set, but it also annoyed her. She still believed in her foul play theory, which the coppers had so quickly discarded, which meant she'd have to work extra hard to find a useful nugget of information.

"Ah, please come in, Miss Halliwell. We've saved the best for last," one clearly enamored officer exclaimed as the rising star sat in the chair facing them.

"What a horrendous day," Clover sniffled in her high-pitched voice as she positioned herself comfortably in her seat to conceal her growing bump with her oversized shawl. She noticed Annabelle out of the corner of her eye and gave her a polite nod, which allowed the new publicity assistant to notice the actress's red nose and bloodshot eyes. She'd been crying quite a bit.

"We'll keep this brief then. Could you tell us where you were on the soundstage and what you were doing when the power went out?" the lead officer asked with surprising tenderness.

"I was sitting in my chair over to the right of the sets.

There was another delay, so everyone was standing by. Miss Stonewood was fetching me a cup of water when the power went out which was shortly followed by that atrocious scream." Clover's voice wavered precariously but she managed to compose herself.

"Did you know the victim, Chuck Thorne, personally? Did you notice him up there prior to the loss of power?" another officer asked with, once again, a newfound warmth which hadn't been used in any other interrogation.

"I didn't know him personally, but I did see him amongst other crew members on set." Clover's baby voice dipped slightly lower than usual. "I'm afraid I don't often think of looking up there. I'm often very focused on my lines and the lighting balcony rarely crosses my mind."

"That's understandable," the lead officer concluded. "We appreciate you taking the time to talk with us, Miss Halliwell. Have a nice evening."

MGM's latest rising star gave Annabelle a half-hearted smile as she listened to her rehearsed publicity speech then left the soundstage in a daze. Annabelle turned to the coppers, who were now only concerned about which restaurant had the best steak in the city instead of going over the interrogations—particularly this last one.

Clover had seemed highly emotional to her. Granted, she had witnessed a death and she was also pregnant—both these being valid reasons for her behaviour. Everyone on the studio lot and in the press were raving about her acting abilities, yet it seemed she could barely reign in these emotions for a crew member she didn't know. Things weren't adding up for Annabelle.

"Well, gentlemen." She stood up, not bothering with a

41

goodbye. They wouldn't truly pay attention to her even if she slapped them across the face.

"Mr. Beauregard is probably waiting impatiently for my feedback," Annabelle mumbled as she once again trekked from one end of the lot to the other.

This day had been an overload of emotions and information, and it still wasn't done with this emergency press conference looming over them. Maybe she was imagining things and Clover Halliwell wasn't acting strangely at all. She didn't know her that well, maybe this was how she reacts to tough situations. She'd have to think about it some more.

"This has been a whopper of a second day on the job." Annabelle exhaled. "How am I even supposed to condense this mess for my weekly letter back home?"

Chapter 9

The second Annabelle walked into the publicity building Nelson dragged her into his office for a debriefing of the interviews. To her surprise, he seemed to relax a bit more with every word she said.

"That's good news. It sounds like no one is brewing up another version of events." Nelson exhaled, rubbing a scruffy hand against his temple. "But we're not out of the woods yet. We need to be on our toes even more—we wouldn't want Miss Halliwell's secret being revealed because of this mess."

"That would be terrible." *Especially if she has more than one secret under wraps,* Annabelle thought. "But as I've said before, I'm here to help if anything comes up."

"Splendid! Well, our next order of business is to get this press conference over and done with. This'll be a treat for you. Press conferences are how we squash bigger issues, so pay close attention," Nelson said as he snatched an official folder from his desk and waved at his new employee to follow him. "Now let's get a move on."

Nelson Beauregard power walked all the way to the MGM front gates with Annabelle nearly running to keep up. The security guard let them through, and they left the studio confines only to turn left and join a rather large crowd on a well-manicured grassy area bordered by luscious plants and bright flowers. Right away she recognized the trio of reporters from the day before amongst the crowd, salivating for new information.

"Now, stay out of the way and don't utter a word. Just listen and learn," Nelson instructed her before joining officers and other executives at the front of the gathering where a small podium was set up. Other than the high hats heading the proceeding and herself, Annabelle didn't recognize anyone as having been present at the accident, let alone another studio employee. It was just a sea of rabid reporters.

"Good afternoon! Thank you for waiting. As you know it's been quite an eventful day." Nelson's loud voice carried just fine without a megaphone, making reporters up front jump back at the volume. "As you're all aware, Miss Halliwell's latest picture, *The Enchantress*, started filming today. Unfortunately, something terrible has happened which halted production.A death."

Gasps and murmurs spread out amongst members of the press. They most likely got wind through the grapevine that something serious had occurred on set without knowing the extent of it. Annabelle thought Mr. Beauregard was making a show of delivering the news dramatically, which she felt was in poor taste. This wasn't another screenplay being pitched to Irving Thalberg after all. This was someone's life that came to an abrupt end!

"One of MGM's crew members in the lighting department, Chuck Thorne, fell to his death from a soundstage balcony. There was nothing to be done once he was found on the ground, it was too late." Nelson added a sombre tone to his voice, but the ridiculous volume at which he talked made it sound garishly theatrical.

"Did anyone see him fall?" a reporter barked.

"No, there was a strange power outage moments before it happened. By all accounts a bloodcurdling scream was heard, and the lights came back on not long after. It all happened in a matter of minutes," Nelson explained before stepping aside to make room for LAPD's lead officer. "Now I'll let the Los Angeles Police Department have a word. They've been working tirelessly all day on this."

"Thank you, Mr. Beauregard. My officers conducted a thorough examination of the body and the soundstage. Then we proceeded with extensive interrogations of every cast and crew member present at the time of the fall. After collecting all the necessary information, we have assessed that this was a tragic accident. It is our theory that the unexplained power outage startled him, making this seasoned lighting technician lose his balance and fall off the balcony," the lead officer announced as all the reporters hunched over their notepads, writing down every word.

Annabelle expected the members of the press to launch into a million questions, but they seemed oddly satisfied with the information provided. Was it because this accident involved a lowly crew member and not one of MGM's popular marquee names? She was baffled that everyone thought this was an open-and-shut case.

"We assure you that MGM is taking all necessary precautions to ensure that the soundstage balconies are sturdy and safe.

Mr. Thorne's wife has been notified. We send her our deepest condolences and have offered to pay for all funeral costs. As Louis B. Mayer himself says, we're a big family here at MGM and we will do everything we can to prevent any further tragic accidents from happening." Nelson discreetly encroached on the officer's space to deliver this message. "And not to worry, the filming of *The Enchantress* will go on as scheduled. This will surely be another hit for Miss Halliwell and MGM!"

And with that overly chipper note, the reporters dispersed, going back to their offices to type up a quick article about a crew member's accidental death on this prestigious lot. They probably wouldn't think about it ever again and it made Annabelle feel more than uneasy.

"See? You gotta keep it short and simple: deliver the bad news but then spin it into a positive message for the studio and the public," Nelson said as he approached his new employee with a satisfied grin. "And now we can go about our business and the coppers will be out of our hair."

"It seemed quite effective," Annabelle noted as she followed her boss back through the studio gates.

"And how! You'll get the hang of it soon enough," Nelson exclaimed as they reached their building. "Well, good work today. I'll see you bright and early tomorrow morning."

He gave Annabelle a hearty pat on the shoulder like she was one of his buddies before turning on his heels. In a trance, she collected her purse, mumbled a goodbye to Ginny and started on her journey home.

Her brain seemed to be at capacity in terms of information and emotions, today's overload weighing her entire body down as she boarded the Red Car. The coppers were eager to close this case and shrug it off, the studio was concerned with saving face and keeping up a pristine reputation, while the press were always on the prowl for *the* juiciest gossip. Clearly, this didn't measure up as such in their eyes.

But what about Chuck Thorne? Didn't he deserve a proper investigation into his death? And what about Clover Halliwell's behaviour? Didn't it strike anyone else as misplaced? Despite being known as a polite and polished gal back in Texas and on the pageant circuit, Annabelle was tenacious when she wanted to see something through. Even though she was new to this role and didn't want to overstep her bounds, it was clear to her that she'd do whatever was necessary to get to the bottom of this mystery.

"It's probably best that my coworkers underestimate me," Annabelle sighed as she hopped off the Red Car. "That way I can snoop around discreetly while keeping my wholesome image intact. It's a win-win!"

Chapter 10

For the first time since she moved into this apartment building, Annabelle was grateful that she didn't cross paths with any of the other tenants. She made herself a sad bowl of oatmeal which she brought up to her room, where she ate it sitting cross-legged on her bed. She couldn't bear the idea of staying up for a moment longer. No radio programs or books by Daphne du Maurier, Dashiell Hammett, or Agatha Christie could possibly interest her this evening.

Calling an early night for the second day in a row, Annabelle washed her face and put on her comfy pyjamas before closing the blinds and crawling into bed. She looked forward to shutting her brain off for the night after an overstimulating day. And it worked. For a short while.

The Stonewoods were known as deep sleepers and Annabelle luckily got a few hours of just that as she lay motionless in her bed. But then she was plopped into a weird limbo shifting between a dream and a nightmare, the primary location being that dreaded soundstage.

"Not this darn set again," she exclaimed, realizing she was conscious of being in a dream state. That was new to her.

But her body seemed to be calling the shots, and before she

knew what was happening, Annabelle's legs walked her all the way to the water cooler. Everything seemed as it was in real life: the frenzied energy and anticipation on the first day of a new shoot. As expected, that red prop book fell to the ground, and just as it happened in real life, she went to pick it up. However, once she and the other dames made contact with it, the dream shifted away from the factual events.

The power outage occurred but Annabelle was surrounded by dead silence instead of the surprised exclamations of the cast and crew. All she could hear was her own breathing and heartbeat.

"Well, this is a little unsettling," she laughed nervously, too creeped out to move an inch. Then she felt a strong vibration. "What now, an earthquake? This day was troubling enough as is."

It took her a moment, but Annabelle realized the vibration wasn't coming from the ground or her surroundings. It was coming from her. Her body was thrumming with an inordinate amount of energy and before long she noticed a yellow mist emanating off her.

"Should my doctor know about this?" She couldn't help cracking jokes, it was too odd even for a dream.

As the delirium set in, she noticed three other sets of coloured mist floating about. The green, orange, purple, and her own yellow mist all floated in separate corners, minding their own business. But it's once the whispers started that they all converged as one, swirling about into a thick tornado with Annabelle trapped inside.

She crouched down and covered her ears, trying to shield herself from the forceful mist and ear-piercing whispers.

49

"Wake up, WAKE UP!" Annabelle yelled, on the verge of tears. She knew this nightmare was all a figment of her imagination, but she couldn't help feeling frightened and frantic.

As if listening to her cries, the mist stood still, and the insect-like whispering stopped. Annabelle stood up slowly, staring into the hypnotic colours floating in front of her. In the blink of an eye, the mist surged forward and collided with her, knocking her to the ground.

"What the devil is happening?" Once again terrified, Annabelle scrambled to her feet, now noticing the four mists penetrated through her skin and glowed through her. "Oh, heavens! This can't be good!"

Her fear subsided as the power came back on and the factual sequence of events unfolded as she observed it all, still glowing. Annabelle relived the rest of the day from a floating bird's-eye view, going through the discovery of the body all the way to the disappointing press conference. But just as she thought her subconscious mind would let her drop back into a deep sleep, instead it catapulted her back to the beginning.

"All right, who's playing a joke on me?" Annabelle stomped her foot on the ground as she was once again on the power-less soundstage with the mists starting to materialize.

She was now stuck in a loop, a deranged merry-go-round which wouldn't let her off, forcing her to live through this day over and over again. No new information was coming to her, but she did feel like her body was being infused with a new, tingly energy every time the mists absorbed through her skin, and somehow that part felt calming to her the more she experienced it.

After what felt like an eternity, the loop stopped with no warning. Instead, Annabelle abruptly woke up, jolting upright in bed with a gasp. Completely disoriented, she was drenched in sweat and light was already streaming through her flimsy blinds.

"Oh, thank goodness," she sputtered, noticing no colourful glow emanating through her skin. She leaned her head in her hands, trying to steady her jagged breathing. "I would have had a lot of explaining to do. Did someone lace my oatmeal with something?"

She spent a whole five seconds debating that theory before her alarm went off, screeching into her ears like a banshee. She turned it off with a smack and a grunt. This dream-nightmare loop had gone on *all night.* Perfect.

Annabelle reached for the glass of water on her bedside table and chugged it. She felt like she had been doing cartwheels for ten hours straight. Her hand shook as she placed the glass back down. All those years touring for pageants taught her how to deal with exhaustion, but this was a whole other beast. This felt more than bone deep, it felt like her body and her mind would never be the same.

"Jiminy Christmas, I don't know if any amount of caffeine will help me get through this day," she whimpered, tossing her legs over the side of the bed. "But here goes nothing."

Chapter 11

If Annabelle didn't know any better, she'd think she was still in that warped dream. It was laughable really, it all felt like an underwater funhouse. Her ride on the Red Car was a muffled blur, she had then managed to get through the studio gate with its stone-faced security guard, and now she found herself face-to-face with Ginny in the publicity building.

"Gee, Miss Stonewood, you look awfully tired." Ginny was staring at her with genuine concern.

"It wasn't a restful night I can tell ya that much," she replied. "And please, call me Annabelle."

"Aha! There you are," Nelson exclaimed as he burst through the door, as if she wasn't on time and in the exact place she was supposed to be. "I have a laundry list of things for you to do this morning. Do you think you can handle it?"

"As long as it's not actual laundry," Annabelle replied with forceful cheeriness, winking at Ginny before following her boss into his office. Maybe if she forced the peppiness, it would infuse some actual energy into her drained body.

The day had only started yet Mr. Beauregard's office already reeked of cigarettes; the sunlight peeked through the window and showed off the smoke that clung to the air. Usually,

Annabelle could stomach it—she didn't smoke herself, but most people did—but today it made her want to pinch her nose and cover her mouth.

"The fellas and I are so busy putting out fires left and right that this has fallen off our list of priorities. But now that you've joined the team, this task seems right up your alley." He handed her a thick portfolio which she had to cling to with two hands. "According to Mayer and other executives, this is our latest crop of MGM fresh faces that should be making waves in the upcoming months. I've compiled a bunch of studio photos and information about them, and I want you to craft the perfect star images for them."

"You want me to create likeable personas for them? Like you did with Gable the all-American man and Harlow the blonde bombshell?" Annabelle asked tentatively. She felt slightly wobbly on her feet and the extra weight of this portfolio wasn't helping.

"You're right on the money!" Nelson smacked a thick hand on his expensive mahogany desk. "Now these kids are really green, no one knows them yet. I'm trusting you to write up celebrity personas for them and then you'll pitch them to the rest of the team. These images we craft at the publicity level are of the utmost importance, it can really dictate the trajectory of someone's career, you know? If the rest of us like what you come up with, we'll go ahead and write up some press releases to send over to the fan magazines to get the ball rolling. Now go ahead and get to work, we want to see some concrete ideas after lunch!"

"I'll get right to it then." Annabelle nodded then hurried over to her office where she plopped the portfolio down with a loud thud.

There was a twinge of panic somewhere deep down, but her sheer exhaustion overrode it. She opened the portfolio and quickly skimmed through it to get a general idea of what she was working with. It wasn't much. There were a lot of studio pictures of a handful of hopeful, fresh-faced actors and actresses, but very little factual information about them other than short lists of motion pictures they had appeared in as bit players along with their height and weight.

"Well, ain't that swell," Annabelle huffed. "I'm supposed to create star-worthy images with this? Might as well be a bunch of newborns. How the heck did executives determine these were our next rising stars anyway? I wouldn't be able to point them out on this lot, it's just a few amongst a sea of pretty faces."

Annabelle allowed herself another two minutes to rant, then she got herself a cup of black coffee, sat down, and began brainstorming. She didn't have time to dillydally, especially when she was only working at less than half her usual spitfire capacity. She had always been disciplined and savvy and she behaved no differently with this task. By the time noon rolled around, her waste basket was filled with crumpled-up papers but thankfully she had decent outlines to pitch.

"Well thanks for hanging in there, old pal," she sighed, tenderly massaging her temples. "I didn't think we had it in us today, but we pulled through somehow."

Once Annabelle's brain released the task, her stomach started growling like a hungry lion. She walked out to the front desk but was disappointed to notice Ginny wasn't sat at her chair. She would have asked the secretary to join her for lunch, but it looked like it would be a solitary affair today. Maybe it was for the best, after exerting her mind over the past few hours, she didn't know if she'd be able to keep up a conversation until she had some food in her.

Making the trek to the commissary, Annabelle had to make a conscious effort to walk like a normal person. It was already bad enough that the publicity department had to squash multiple stories about stars and their day drinking; she didn't want to look like she was zozzled on the job. She never did it during pageants and she wouldn't be starting that nonsense now.

As usual the commissary was filled with conversations at high volume, everyone trying to one-up each other with stories about their day on set. Annabelle got in line, picked up a ham and brie sandwich with some coleslaw, then found herself a secluded spot at the very end of a long cafeteria-length table.

She zoned out as she ate, only coming to when her hands were empty. She allowed herself some time for people-watching; no one could fault her for that at *the* prestige studio. Who else could say they had lunch in close proximity to Myrna Loy? The energy in the commissary was as exciting as all those soundstages.

Speaking of which, Annabelle saw a flash of long, curly black hair slither along the wall opposite her. It was only when the woman turned around that she realized it was one of the other three women who had tried picking up that prop book just as the power went out yesterday on the soundstage.

"Come to think of it, I don't recall seeing this dame during the interrogations ... or the two others for that matter," Annabelle mumbled, getting up before she had a plan of action.

She took a few steps, hoping to have a brief conversation with the woman in question, when a man stepped out in her path and stared her down. It was one of the older fellas from her new department and he looked like he was in a teasing mood.

"Well looks like Miss Pageant Queen thinks she's allowed an extra-long lunch break," the man smirked. His name was either Bernard, Robert, or Chester but Annabelle couldn't remember. What she did know was that he seemed somehow insulted that the publicity department hired someone with a feminine touch. As a matter of fact, he seemed to take personal offense at it. "How about you get back to work sweetheart? We don't want no slackers or delicate flowers that can't do the tough work."

"I've been gone half an hour at most but don't worry, I expect to dazzle the team with my pitch this afternoon." She gave him a closed-mouthed smile. No one around them seemed to be paying much attention, which was probably for the best. The amount of masculine power trips around here was most likely in the triple digits.

She tried to circle him, still wanting to talk with the raven-haired mystery woman, but this guy wouldn't budge. He just kept on making rude remarks and getting in her way. Annabelle felt anger flaring up within her and the slight pulse of a headache was coming on. This bozo was getting on her last nerve.

Just at that moment, a commissary employee was approaching them with a pitcher full of water, and all Annabelle wanted to do was to pour that pitcher over this idiot. As if on cue, the pitcher jerked out of the employee's hand and spilled all over whatshisname. Annabelle took a step back and stifled a giggle. What a convenient coincidence!

"You clumsy fool! Fetch me a towel NOW," her colleague bellowed at the poor employee.

Guilty that the employee now had to deal with this guy's attitude problem, but also grateful the attention had been deflected off of her, Annabelle slipped around the table and scanned the room. The woman she set her sights on wasn't there anymore.

"Rats," she grumbled as she exited the commissary, shielding her eyes so she could take a look around. There was no trace of those long black curls anywhere.

Annabelle was surprised by how disappointed she was. It was probably an oversight that this dame hadn't been questioned; maybe she had only been dropping something off on behalf of whatever department she worked for and wasn't scheduled to be on set. Either way, she felt the need to track her down and talk to her. There might be a slight possibility she knew something about the deceased that would come in handy. But that would be a problem for another day.

"Oh, brother that was a laugh," Annabelle giggled as she thought about the water pitcher incident from moments ago. The headache that had sprouted in that moment was now fully formed and screaming at her in the sunlight. "I desperately need some shade and aspirin. And I need to ace that pitch. That's all I can focus on today."

Chapter 12

After having pitched some stellar star personas for a bunch of up-and-coming MGM contract players, Annabelle's colleagues reluctantly agreed that her ideas were up to snuff. Just as she had expected, her ability to craft an image based on perception had come in handy. Feeling satisfied that she managed to complete this complex task after a hellish night, Annabelle was grateful that she was slowly earning her place amongst the publicity department and that she'd hopefully be considered for bigger assignments.

But when she reported for duty the next day, feeling decidedly more refreshed and like herself, it seemed like her great work from the day before had been forgotten.

"*The Enchantress* is about to start filming again so you'll be needed to shadow Miss Halliwell. The press are after her like hounds, trying to get a quote from her about the accident, and I wouldn't put it past those scoundrels to get on the lot under false pretenses and try to sneak on her soundstage. You'll have to be eagle-eyed today and hopefully the interest will tamper down soon," Nelson explained as he lit another cigarette and waved her away. "Off you go!"

Annabelle nodded enthusiastically before turning on her

heels and starting the familiar trek to the soundstage. Part of her was disappointed that she was assigned to this babysitting role again after having shown her abilities yesterday. But then she realized this would be the perfect opportunity to get a better read on Clover Halliwell and her devastated reaction following the accident. Annabelle was a good judge of character and spending more time around the actress was definitely necessary at this point in her digging.

"If only Mr. Beauregard knew this assignment was twofold," Annabelle said in a sing-song voice as she hopped off the trolley and stood in front of the soundstage.

She understood logistically, financially, and schedule-wise that they had to keep using the original soundstage where poor Chuck Thorne fell to his death for filming. Studios were a well-oiled machine, and every inch of space was used efficiently. But still, it gave Annabelle the heebie-jeebies setting foot in there again when someone lay dead on the floor only a few days prior.

She opened the door and stepped inside, surprised the atmosphere felt the same as it had on the first morning. The employees of various departments were bustling about, making sure all details were at perfection level, but she could sense a serious undercurrent. Annabelle found the leading lady in the same spot as last time, on her chair to the left of the sets with a vacant look in her eyes.

"Good mornin', Miss Halliwell! Fancy seeing you here," Annabelle chirped, hoping the cheery tone would pull the actress out of her slump.

"Oh, hello Annabelle, I didn't see you there." The sparkle in Clover's blue eyes was not present today and she looked absolutely exhausted. She didn't look like she belonged on the set of a picture at all, and it made Annabelle panic a little bit.

"Do you want me to practice lines with you? It looks like they need to finish setting things up," Annabelle offered.

"No that's all right, I know them well enough." Clover waved a limp hand at her. "I just want filming to get underway already."

That's when the director busted out his megaphone again, a sheepish look on his face.

"Well folks it looks like we have a sound problem that needs tending to. We don't know how long it'll take so you can leave the soundstage and we'll call you back in a few hours." The director's announcement elicited groans from the cast and crew. "I promise, day one of filming will get underway later today!"

"Fiddlesticks!" Clover stood up from her chair and stomped her foot before remembering to properly shield her growing belly. "That's just what I needed today. Say, would you like to join me in my dressing room? I'd love the company."

"Only if it's not an imposition," Annabelle replied. The invitation surprised her since Clover seemed pos-i-tutely morose and cranky, but this one-on-one time would be rare to come by.

"Of course not! Follow me." Clover guided Annabelle outside and off the side of the building where a driver was waiting for her in a cart. "To my dressing room, please."

It was a slow ride, weaving through all the cast and crew that had just vacated the soundstage unexpectedly, but five minutes later they found themselves in front of the ladies' apartments.

"I had one of those small, portable dressing rooms up until recently, and now I have one of those big rooms," Clover explained as they climbed up the stairs. "I guess it means I'm doing something right."

"I'll say!" Annabelle exclaimed, never having come close to this building. The extras always had to do costume changes in the most random locations and never had a place of their own to lie down on the studio lot. And from the looks of it, the same could be said for the publicity department.

As Clover was unlocking her door, a glamourous neighbour was opening theirs. Annabelle stood there, starstruck as Greta Garbo herself locked her dressing room, gave them an almost imperceptible nod, and walked away.

"Well I'll be damned, Garbo is in the room right next to yours?" Annabelle knew she wasn't coming across as professional, but she couldn't help herself. That dame was more than magnetic.

"Isn't it a laugh? She's the quietest actress on the lot, I can tell you that much. I'm terribly curious about what she has in her room, but she's never invited me over." Clover shrugged as she opened her door. "Ta-dah! Isn't it spiffy? I know it isn't the biggest one around but I'm quite proud of it."

"It's lovely," Annabelle mused as she looked around. There was a living room area with plush couches around a table, then beyond that there was a makeup chair facing a brightly lit mirror and partitions to change. It wasn't half bad for a star on the up-and-up.

"Geez Louise, who knew pregnancy made your feet swell this much?" Clover sighed as she sat down on the couch and took off her shoes. "How about we play some gin rummy to kill the time?"

"With pleasure." Annabelle sat opposite her and shuffled the deck of cards already poised for play on the coffee table.

It turned out they were both pretty competitive and were fully intent on beating each other, which kept Clover in high spirits. But it's once the game was over that her sombre attitude returned.

"I can't help but ask ..." Annabelle cleared her throat, hoping she wouldn't get booted out of the dressing room for asking this. "You seemed very torn up about Chuck Thorne's death during the interrogations. If I can say so, you seemed to be the only one who was genuinely upset."

"Well, it was rather tragic, and my current predicament is making me all out of sorts." Clover averted her gaze as she caressed her stomach, her normally breathy voice turning scratchy.

"That's understandable. Did you know him?" Annabelle prodded, hopefully not on the verge of crossing a line.

"I'd seen him around." Clover's voice was wobbly, like she was trying to hold something back. She could act perfectly in front of a camera while in character but when it came time to expressing herself in person, she was a lousy liar.

"I don't want to seem presumptuous, but I have a feeling there's more to the story," Annabelle asked tentatively. "I've already been entrusted with this secret pregnancy. Surely you know I have your best interests at heart."

Clover mulled it over for a second before bursting into tears, her hands cradling her belly protectively.

"Oh applesauce, I can't keep this in anymore!" Clover blubbered. "Chuck and I were seeing each other secretly. And yes, I'm aware he has a wife, but Chuck told me their marriage was all for show. We were in love and now he's gone! I don't know what to do with myself."

"I take it he's the father?" Annabelle asked. This onslaught of information confirmed her suspicions but didn't simplify a thing. "Did his wife know about your affair?"

"Yes, he is," Clover hiccupped. "I haven't the slightest clue if she knows but why would it matter now with him gone?"

"This might sound a bit mad, but I have reason to believe Chuck's death wasn't an accident," Annabelle said slowly, not wanting to send this poor pregnant actress into a fit.

"What do you mean? The police said it was an accident." Clover's bloodshot eyes focused on her.

"I noticed some big bruises on his arms that seemed consistent with hand marks. I tried telling the coppers, but they dismissed it, wanting an open and closed case," Annabelle explained as she got up and went to sit right next to Clover, petting her on the knee. "I'm sorry to bombard you with all this information, I know it's a lot to process."

"I can't believe this," Clover's voice had gone hard. "So, you're telling me you think Chuck was *pushed* off the balcony? How horrible."

"I know it's not my responsibility, but I hate the idea of the truth being buried. I'm going to need your cooperation on this, and we'll need to keep it hush-hush," Annabelle said as she took charge. "I'm no private eye but we need to find out if Mrs. Thorne knew about your affair, regardless of the state of their marriage. Because if she did, that's a darn good motive for murdering her husband."

Chapter 13

Needless to say, after that whopper of a confession, Annabelle had trouble focusing on the task at hand. As expected, filming on *The Enchantress* resumed about an hour and a half later and all the cast and crew reported back to set. She had to hand it to Clover, she acted beautifully for the camera even though she was distressed under the veils of her makeup and costume.

When she arrived in Los Angeles as a bright-eyed and bushy-tailed extra, Annabelle was positively in awe of filmmaking. From the sets to the camera all the way to the scrip revisions being brought in at the last second, she was mesmerized by all of it. And although she was still entranced by all these elements coming together, heck that's why she didn't hitch a ride back to Texas after her extra days were over, there was something about seeing take after take of Joan Crawford slugging someone in the face that brought it back down to earth and made it seem like everyday work.

She stared at Clover from her hiding spot off the side of the stage, watching her interact with the other actors and the scenery and all Annabelle could think about was the predicament this actress was in. It was already bad enough trying to conceal a pregnancy out of wedlock, but it turns out the father was a married fella who may just have been pushed to his death on set. It was a pretty big pickle.

"Thank you all for your patience. We got in a solid eight hours of work," the director announced in his megaphone after yelling "cut" on the final scene of the day. "I'll see you all bright and early tomorrow."

A procession of exhausted employees started shuffling out, relieved the day was over. Annabelle hung back, waiting for the lead actress to finish her conversation with her fellow cast members. They were probably around the same age, but Annabelle felt a strange mix of admiration and protectiveness toward Clover.

"You didn't have to wait for me you know? I can get to my dressing room like a big girl," Clover half-heartedly teased as she approached her.

"I just wanted to make sure you didn't need anything else from me today." Annabelle shrugged.

"No, I should be all right," Clover sighed, protectively crossing her arms over her stomach. She looked dead tired, the layers of pancake makeup which had been on her face all day now no longer concealing the deep, dark circles under her eyes. "Besides, as far as I know you're not my personal assistant! You don't need to dote on me."

"Well, I feel like I'm everyone's assistant sometimes," Annabelle laughed. "I know it's been a rough day and I want you to know I'm here to help. Just holler for me and I'll come running."

"Gee, Annabelle, that's very kind of you." Clover reached out and gave her hand a squeeze. "You know, everyone is telling me my star is on the rise and that I'm constantly in demand. But it can feel pretty lonely sometimes ... Can I trust you to keep our conversation between us?"

"Of course." Annabelle nodded. "You can count on me."

"You're the berries! Have a nice evening." Clover gave her a wave as she walked toward the soundstage exit.

Annabelle hung around for a few minutes longer, staring up at the lighting balcony and its surroundings before leaving. The sun was setting, and she decided to take the long way to the publicity building; her workday was over, but she wasn't in a rush to get home. Despite an onslaught of studio employees being done for the day, a whole other wave of them were only getting started. Many Spanish-language versions of MGM pictures were filmed on set at night and their own cast and crews were getting ready to work, making the entire studio alive twenty-four hours a day.

Annabelle kept a leisurely pace while staying out of everyone's way, but her mind was racing. Was it wise to keep this secret affair to herself? Would it help if she told Mr. Beauregard in case the publicity department needed to spin the story if it was leaked?

"Maybe I should keep it to myself for now," Annabelle mumbled as she strolled behind some outdoor sets of a small European village. "I need to view this from beyond my standing as a member of the publicity department. This could all be linked to a murder. It happened on the studio lot after all, we wouldn't want this information getting into the wrong hands."

She had come to learn that secrets weren't always *secret knowledge* around here—people often traded them like they were up for grabs. But something told her Clover Halliwell kept things close to her chest. The fact that only Mr. Beauregard, and not

66

the rest of the publicity team, knew about her illicit pregnancy was rather telling. The department could basically be renamed the "chamber of secrets" and yet this one hadn't slithered in.

"That settles it then," Annabelle decided. "I'll only tell if absolutely necessary."

She turned a corner and was approaching an outdoor set, which looked like a half-built storefront in shambles, where two people were having a conversation. It's only once they turned to acknowledge her presence that she realized that it was none other than Irving Thalberg and his wife Norma Shearer, a.k.a MGM's top producer and queen of the lot. Annabelle gave them a courteous nod then noticed in horror a huge plank of wood falling off the top of the set above their heads.

"Look out!" Annabelle yelled as she flailed her arms.

The strangest thing happened before they had time to react. Annabelle felt a tingly feeling all over as she saw the plank veer away from them mid-air, as if being pulled by an invisible force, and smash to the ground a few feet away as they jumped back.

"Jeepers, that was a close one! You really saved our necks," Norma gasped, holding a manicured hand to her chest.

"What's your name?" Irving asked sternly, making Annabelle think she was in trouble somehow.

"M-my name is Annabelle Stonewood. I'm a new publicity assistant," she answered shakily.

"A dame in that department? You don't say! Well, I'll let Nelson know he has a very alert employee working for him." He reached out and gave her a firm handshake. "Thanks again Miss Stonewood, I'll give the set department a good talking to. Things shouldn't be falling off like that. Let's go, dear, we have dinner plans with Helen Hayes and her husband."

As the famous couple walked away, Annabelle stood by the dilapidated set, shellshocked. They hadn't seen it with their own eyes, but she had. She had felt the same tingly sensation throughout her body moments before that pitcher of water was dumped on her idiot colleague in the commissary. She had thought that incident was a comical coincidence, but now ...

"Am I going crackers, or did I just deviate that plank of wood right out of the air?" Annabelle asked out loud, no one around to answer for her as she looked at her hands in confusion.

Chapter 14

Annabelle once again found herself trying to make the security guard at the front gate crack a smile. She felt like she had only left the studio a few hours before yet here she found herself again. After yesterday's bizarre antics with the wood plank that nearly landed on some very famous heads, she wracked her brain trying to come up with a logical explanation for what she saw. The only one she could come up with was that her mind was playing tricks on her. After all, she did work at one of the country's most prestigious motion picture studios where it was their job to conjure up wildly extravagant scenarios for the viewing public, *and* an actual murder had occurred on set only a few days prior. No wonder her imagination was going wonky.

"At least I didn't have one of those active dreams again. That was a doozy," she muttered as she approached the front door of the publicity department, when a familiar voice made her spin around.

"Ah, Miss Stonewood! You're going the wrong way." Nelson wagged a teasing finger at her, his booming voice making it sound more like a scolding than playful, but Annabelle was starting to get used to his humour. "I need you to go down to the wardrobe department. They picked out some costumes and since you were excellent at coming up with personas, I need you to confirm if they fit together."

"All right, I'll get right to it Mr. Beauregard." Annabelle gave him an excited wave as she turned around. Either he truly believed she was right for this task, or he just wanted her out of his hair, but she didn't care. She hadn't had the chance to hang around the wardrobe department that much, but it sounded so fun and lively. "I'll make sure the outfits match them to a T!"

"Yeah, yeah," Nelson smirked, a new cigarette dangling out of his mouth. "Now skedaddle!"

Even though she had a lot on her plate, Annabelle was looking forward to this task. Choosing outfits made her think of her pageant days fondly, with all the tassels, cowboy boots, and bathing suits in bright colours. Her heart pinched for a moment, wanting to go back to those simpler times. But she knew she had outgrown that circuit and was ready for something new and challenging. And boy did she find it.

Annabelle finally made it to the wardrobe building and as expected it was hectic. There were racks and racks of beautiful gowns and suits being rolled around, with frenzied seamstresses scurrying about.

"Excuse me, I'm supposed to approve some wardrobe items? Mr. Beauregard sent me over from the publicity department," Annabelle asked who she assumed was the receptionist hovering by the front desk.

"Oh yes, follow me." The woman led her down a hall to a back room with clothes hung up all the way to the ceiling. It was the biggest closet Annabelle had ever seen. "We set some selections aside over on that rack. Take your time and let me know if you need anything."

"Perfect, thank you," Annabelle replied.

"One last thing." The receptionist turned to face her again, giving her a sheepish look. "Please don't swipe any of the clothes. Sometimes people find excuses to come in here and touch the suits Clark Gable wore, or the mink coats Jeanette MacDonald drapes over her shoulders, and some have even snuck out wearing the outfits! Us gals need to make disclaimers now: if you get caught, you get canned."

"Well, isn't that silly," Annabelle laughed loudly, surprising both of them. "Some people do the darnedest things! There's no need to worry about me, honey, I intend on staying employed."

With that sorted, the receptionist left her alone in that big outfit warehouse with a clear conscience. Annabelle walked up to the rack, happy that someone had clipped pictures of the actors in question to refresh her memory about their assigned star personas. She took her time looking at each outfit and really thinking about how it would come across. Then she'd set aside what worked to one side of the rack and what didn't to the other.

"Who would have known I'd be approving outfits for up-and-coming actresses?" Annabelle chuckled to herself, or so she thought. She saw movement out of the corner of her eye then jumped back when she noticed someone hovering in the doorway. "Jeepers! I didn't see you there."

"I'm terribly sorry. I didn't mean to frighten you." The woman seemed rather shy, not knowing if she should enter the room or scram. She eventually slowly tiptoed in and went off to the right where she analyzed a bunch of palazzo pants lying flat on a sewing table.

"You look familiar." Annabelle turned to look at her; she had seen those long raven tresses before. Specifically on the set of *The Enchantress* and in the commissary before the pitcher incident. "I take it you work in wardrobe?"

"Yes," the woman answered quietly, eyes still on the pants.

"Did you happen to be on the soundstage of Clover Halliwell's latest movie when the lighting technician fell?" Annabelle asked bluntly, which is not a tone she enjoyed using but she felt it necessary to speed up this conversation. "I think I bent down to pick up a book at the same time as you ... then it was lights out."

The woman turned and stared at her for a long time. She seemed to be pondering what to say. "Am I in trouble? I was simply dropping off Miss Halliwell's latest outfit when I saw the book fall."

"Heavens no! Where are my southern manners." Annabelle started over with a more jovial approach. "My name is Annabelle Stonewood and I'm a new publicity assistant. That was my first day on one of the soundstages and it was astonishingly eventful.I didn't catch your name?"

"My name is Milagros Luna, I'm also new to the studio. I started last week," the woman answered, loosening up a smidge."It's very sad what happened to that man."

"It's quite tragic." Annabelle nodded. "Say, I was asked to stick around for the police interrogations, and I don't remember seeing you there. Did you happen to notice anything important before the lights went out?"

"I'm afraid not. As you can tell, I'm rather shy and I tend to keep my head down and get the job done." Milagros shrugged. "I wouldn't have been able to give any pertinent information, anyway, I hadn't even noticed there was a balcony up there.

There were a lot of people on that soundstage."

"Yes, that's the problem," Annabelle replied absentmindedly, already focusing on something else that was nagging at her. "If I remember correctly, there were two other dames who tried scooping up that fallen book. Do you happen to know them?"

"No." Milagros shook her head and Annabelle could sense she was retreating back into her shell at the mention of the book.

"Hmm, I wonder what departments they work for," Annabelle thought out loud, hands on hips. The more she thought about that specific moment where the four of them came in contact with that prop book, the more it became clear that that was the first time she experienced that full-body tingle. Surely, that meant something.

"Well, it was a pleasure meeting you," Milagros said as she slowly shuffled out of the room.

Annabelle was convinced Milagros was holding something back, but she didn't want to push the issue. She desperately wanted to ask her if she had also experienced strange incidents since touching the book which made her feel kooky, but she bit her tongue. Saying it out loud would be taking it a step further than she felt comfortable with.

Chapter 15

Annabelle left the wardrobe department feeling more frazzled than ever. She had perfectly completed the task she was assigned with, all the outfits coordinating with the chosen personas, but her interactions with Milagros didn't clear anything up. Annabelle was grateful she happened to bump into one of the dames who touched the book, but that dame seemed less than willing to talk about it. She seemed pos-i-tutely spooked.

"She clearly doesn't know anything about Chuck's fall, and I should be relieved about that. But *now* I have a million questions swirling around in my mind and it doesn't seem like she'd answer them anytime soon." Annabelle sighed, looking up at the fluffy clouds to centre herself.

What could she do now? Whatever suspicions she had about herself and that prop book still couldn't be answered. She'd have to stumble upon the two other ladies, who also made contact with the book, to have a better understanding of what was going on. That could take a while at a studio that employed thousands of people, but Annabelle was never the type to wait around for things to happen.

"There *is* something I could do but it might get me in trouble." Annabelle bit her lip as she thought it over. "But I'm sure I could wiggle my way out of it is necessary. I'm surprisingly good at playing dumb."

With her mind made up, she ventured over to the human resources building as she came up with a basic plan to get what she wanted. It wasn't a polished plan to her usual standards, but it should do the trick.

"Hello, can I help you with something? If you're looking for more extra work, you're in the wrong building." The woman behind the front desk only briefly glanced up at her and made a nearly spot-on assessment, much to Annabelle's annoyance. Why did people look down on extras? They worked their tails off just as much as everyone else!

"Actually, I'm now with the publicity department," Annabelle replied, holding back the sass so she could ask for a favour. "You see, I've been crafting these star personas for a new batch of up-and-comers and I've been sent over here to review their personal files."

"Is that so? No one has asked for them before." The woman leaned back in her chair and crossed her arms. "What did you say your name was?"

"Annabelle Stonewood." She gave the cranky woman a bright smile. "I suggested we look at their files to make sure our personas match up. You see, we wouldn't want any conflicting information coming to light. It would be horrifying if we spent all this time promoting some new starlet with a refined, worldly background if it's uncovered that her father down in Missouri was a polygamist. The fan magazines would have a field day with such a story! We need to know in advance so we're ready to spin stories the right way. Do you catch my drift?"

The woman simply stared at her with a raised eyebrow, her lips stretched thin. She wasn't buying it. This southern gal would really have to lean into her bluffing.

"Look, we all know Mr. Mayer runs a tight ship with this glitzy studio, all the morality clauses and such. Your files have information that the publicity department can use to avoid ghastly scandals, which will benefit all the employees here. You never know, we could all be one big scandal away from going bust! Stranger things have happened."

The human resources lady was thinking it over. Annabelle had struck a nerve.

"I report to Mr. Beauregard, and he wouldn't be too pleased to know I had trouble accessing these files. He lives and breathes for the publicity department and this studio's fate," Annabelle added for good measure.

"I certainly don't want that loud grump sore at me. He barks instead of speaking," the lady grumbled as she stood up from her rickety chair. "All right, I can fetch those files for you but you gotta make it quick, and I don't want other departments catching wind of this.We aren't a library!"

"Of course." Annabelle nodded then followed the woman to a back room filled with file cabinets.

"Now what were their names?" the woman asked as she opened several cabinets, pulling them out as far as they could go to see the names listed on the files.

Annabelle gave her the names and waited for her back to be turned before conducting her own research.

"I'm from Galveston, Texas and golly is it different from Los Angeles." Annabelle started rambling about her life story, hoping her voice would drown out her own snooping.

She assumed the files were organized alphabetically by surname and luckily, she was right. She opened cabinets only deep enough to catch a peek until she found the letter T.

"... and then her twirling baton caught fire! It was the most dramatic talent show I had ever attended. Naturally the poor dear didn't win the crown," Annabelle guffawed, taking up as much space as she could to hide the opened cabinet behind her back as the woman turned around and stared at her. This dame was either annoyed or enthralled by her pageant stories and it grabbed her attention enough to prevent her from noticing Annabelle's true antics.

The human resources employee sighed and turned back around, hunching over a cabinet with her back turned to this blabbermouth.

Annabelle squinted, saw the name THORNE, and dared to part the file open wide enough for her to find what she was looking for. If she could memorize frivolous speeches for years on end to dazzle pageant judges, she could surely memorize one simple home address. She stared at it long enough for it to imprint in her mind, all the while running her mouth with random stories until she felt confident enough that it was locked in, then she soundlessly closed the cabinet mere seconds before her new confidante turned back around with her own stack of files in her hands.

"Ah, you found them!" Annabelle exclaimed innocently, unsure for a moment if her snooping had been spotted.

"And right on time. Surely, you've exhausted all your life stories by now," the woman quipped. "Now you can go sit at the front office and glean whatever is pertinent for the publicity department, but you cannot leave with these files. Am I understood?"

"As clear as day! Thank you for your help, you've been swell," Annabelle said as she took the files.

She went to her designated seat, almost feeling like she had been scolded by a teacher, and proceeded to jot down what she considered useful. She had to give herself credit, this fake request would make it seem like she went the extra mile for these star personas and hopefully Mr. Beauregard would appreciate that. But she was satisfied that her ultimate goal was completed.

Now that she had an address, Annabelle would pay Mrs. Louise Thorne a personal visit to see if this widow was on the level after all.

Chapter 16

Instead of taking her regular Red Car route to her apartment, Annabelle found herself hopping off in the neighbouring Baldwin Hills area. She befriended a few locals on the ride, and they gave her directions to the location of her unannounced visit.

"Well, here it is, the Thorne residence," she sighed as she double checked the address from her scribbled paper to the numbers painted in bright green paint on the mailbox. "Here goes nothing."

She tucked the paper back in her purse before opening the gate and walking up the path leading to the well-maintained house. It wasn't extravagant by any means, but you could tell by the pristine white paint and immaculate garden that it was well cared for. Annabelle knocked cheerily three times and assessed what type of mood would be perceived from her presence. She was visiting "in a professional capacity" and this woman had just lost her husband, so she couldn't waltz in too bubbly or eager for information. She was already worried this would get back to Mr. Beauregard somehow, so it was of the utmost importance for Annabelle to strike the right tone for this to go over well.

"Yes?" the woman asked after opening the door. She was all done up, her hair and makeup immaculate with an outfit to match.

"Are you Louise Thorne? I'm Annabelle Stonewood from the publicity department at Metro-Goldwyn-Mayer. Am I catching you at a bad time?"

"Oh. No, not at all. I've been getting dressed up out of habit lately. Please come in." Louise moved aside to let her in. The inside of the house looked just as clean and stylish as the outside.

"You have a lovely home," Annabelle exclaimed as she sat down on a cozy burgundy couch. "I dream of someday having a place of my own like this."

"Thank you." Louise's eyes twinkled at the compliment as she sat opposite her guest in a matching chair. But her expression quickly pivoted to sadness. "It's all I have now."

"I'm terribly sorry for your loss. I heard your husband was a loyal employee and a hard worker," Annabelle offered.

"Yeah, and he died because of a silly accident," Louise spat, shaking her head. "I can't believe he's gone."

Annabelle gave Louise a silent moment to blow her nose and dab her eyes with a handkerchief. It didn't seem like Mrs. Thorne suspected anything other than a tragic fall—unless that's just what she wanted people to believe. Either way, Annabelle would keep her mouth shut about her suspicions; she wanted to see how this would play out.

"I apologize, I'm having trouble keeping my composure," Louise sniffled, sitting up straighter. "I wasn't expecting anyone from the studio to stop by."

"Yes, I realize this is sudden." Annabelle cleared her throat.

"Our department worked closely with the police following the tragedy and it occurred to us that we hadn't contacted you to extend our sympathies and expertise. As you know we handle matters with the press regarding the studio and its stars and we wanted to lend you a hand if any reporters were pestering you. I could give you some tips or guidelines to help them run along and leave you alone. They do love to pry in situations like this unfortunately."

"Chuck used to call them vultures," Louise chuckled half-heartedly. "A few of them prowled around for a few hours, but they left real quick when they realized there was no scoop to catch. Chuck and I had a quiet life and marriage, it would be of no interest to the gossip columnists. Besides, he was only a lighting technician—that's a long way down from Marion Davies! The only comment I really made when those reporters showed up was that he looked forward to working on *The Enchantress*. Clover Halliwell is the talk of the town, and he was looking forward to being a small part of her latest project."

"That's understandable." Annabelle nodded as nerves rushed from her toes to her scalp. The way this widow talked fondly about her departed husband and his secret celebrity mistress, she clearly didn't have a clue that an affair was going on behind her back. On the one hand, it made Annabelle re-evaluate her murder theory; maybe it was a fateful accident after all. But on the other hand, she felt an overwhelming sense of guilt at knowing this secret information and was struggling with deciding if it was her place to reveal it or not. It might not be good for her job, but how could she leave this poor grieving woman in the dark? "Mrs. Thorne, you should know that—"

Annabelle lost her ability to speak when she noticed the chair

Louise was sitting on started levitating, then all the objects and furniture in the room started to shake uncontrollably as if they were shivering.

"What in the devil is happening? Is this an earthquake?" Her hostess looked around, seemingly not noticing the slight levitation of her chair, which clearly couldn't be chalked up to an earth-rooted phenomenon.

"How strange!" Annabelle squealed as that familiar full-body tingle took over, making her want to sink into the couch with embarrassment. She closed her eyes and took a few steadying breaths, hoping it would somehow make a difference. And within a matter of seconds, the whole room stilled, and Louise's chair settled back down to the ground with a thud.

"Goodness! That was the most bizarre quake I ever experienced!" Louise seemed to find the whole situation amusing. "I grew up in the Midwest and tornadoes are rather common out there, but California earthquakes are another beast altogether, don't you think?"

"Pos-i-tutely," Annabelle giggled nervously, though annoyed and scared would be a better description of how she felt. She stood up clumsily, the shakes having now settled into her legs. "Well, I don't want to take up anymore of your time. If you ever find yourself in a peculiar situation with the press or if you simply want to talk, just call the publicity department and ask for Annabelle."

"You're leaving so soon? Don't you want to stay for tea?" Louise got up and followed her guest who was already halfway out the front door. "Are you all right? You seem rather pale."

"I'm fine and dandy." Annabelle mustered a smile and an awkward hand flapping motion. "I should get home and make sure my plants and cats aren't too frightened, you know how skittish they can get."

"The plants or the cats?" Louise asked, still somewhat amused.

"The cats, of course! Have a nice evening and thank you for taking the time to talk with me." Annabelle smiled, turned on her heels, and power walked down the street, not daring to glance behind her.

"The poor dear, she must be terrified of earthquakes." Louise shook her head and closed her front door.

Annabelle only slowed her crazed walk once she turned the corner, making sure she was completely out of sight from the Thorne residence before leaning on a tree to catch her breath.

"Horsefeathers! That did not go as planned." Annabelle fanned herself with her free hand despite the chilly spring weather. She was absolutely positive that was not an earthquake; her nerves had caused that spooky scene. "I need to figure out what is going on here. I can't keep looking frazzled and using my imaginary cats as an excuse to scram. How terribly unbecoming!"

Chapter 17

"Please pick up, please pick up." Annabelle tapped her foot on the ground as she held the telephone receiver tight.

"Metro-Goldwyn-Mayer publicity department, how can I help you?" Ginny answered cheerily.

"Hi. Ginny. It's Annabelle. I take it Mr. Beauregard isn't in yet?"

"Good morning! No, he shouldn't be in for another half hour at least. That man is on his own schedule most of the time." Ginny's sigh came out like static on the other end of the line. "Is something wrong?"

"Well, let's just say our boss won't be pleased with me." Annabelle cleared her throat. "I'm feeling a little under the weather ... Stomach issues run in the family. I have to go see a doctor today, so I won't be coming into the studio."

"Oh boy, and you want innocent ole me to deliver the message?" Ginny laughed nervously.

"I feel lousy about it but I'm out of options. I'll bring in a doctor's note tomorrow to smooth things over, maybe even some pastries," Annabelle said. She didn't enjoy lying to Ginny, it made her feel even worse than she already did.

"All right, I hope you feel better soon. See you tomorrow," Ginny replied calmly before hanging up.

They hadn't had a chance to spend much time together, but Annabelle could already sense a camaraderie brewing. They were the only two dames in the department after all, they needed to look out for each other.

She put the receiver back on the telephone in the boarding house's common living room before grabbing her purse and stepping outside. She hopped on the Red Car and paid extra close attention to the stops, not wanting to forget the directions listed on the flyer. Annabelle had a family doctor back in Texas but naturally he couldn't do house calls out in California, so she had to make do with the nearest doctor listed in the newspapers. Hopefully he wasn't an utter quack.

The tramway ride took a little longer than anticipated and she nearly fell asleep with the slight swaying motion. After yesterday's antics in front of Mrs. Thorne, Annabelle hadn't slept a wink and was petrified another *occurrence* would happen at any moment. She didn't have a logical explanation for it so she was hoping a man of medicine would be able to diagnose what was wrong with her, because if she knew one thing, it was that she had caused that "earthquake" and those other little happenings before it.

Once she hopped off the Red Car, she found the address listed in the advertisement on a rather unassuming beige building that looked beyond bland.

"No wonder they need to advertise in the papers with that sad looking storefront," Annabelle mumbled as she walked up the front steps and let herself in.

Apparently, the advertisements performed well because there were at least a dozen people sitting in a crammed waiting room. She announced her presence to the receptionist, citing "troubling stomach issues," then she sat down on the last available chair.

For the first time since she started her new job with the publicity department, Annabelle's brain was devoid of all thoughts. She simply sat there, staring straight ahead at the beige wall, thinking of absolutely nothing as people around her coughed or squirmed in discomfort. Her mind had been in overdrive for too long and it needed to shut off for a while.

"Miss Stonewood, the doctor is ready for you." The receptionist gently touched her arm.

"Jeepers!" Annabelle jumped in her seat before turning toward the clock on the wall, surprised two full hours had passed. "Is that really the time? I can't believe it."

"I thought you were sleeping with your eyes open, but I guess you were deep in thought," the receptionist chuckled as she pointed the way down the hall to the doctor's office.

"That's the problem, I wasn't thinking at all," Annabelle quipped before thanking her.

The doctor was waiting for her, holding open the door to his office. He was a tall man with a big belly and a stern face. He reminded her of a mean version of old Saint Nick. He looked like a no-nonsense sort of man and that's exactly what Annabelle needed.

"What is the matter exactly? My assistant listed your reason for visiting as being due to stomach issues?" The doctor asked as he read from his clipboard.

"It's something along those lines." Annabelle laughed nervously as she paced the small office. "It starts off as a warm feeling in my stomach, then my entire body gets tingly, you

86

see? And it somehow affects gravity and objects around me."

"I beg your pardon?" The doctor's eyes stared at her.

"Have you ever heard of stomach issues that can cause things to move of their own accord?" Annabelle asked as she traced a finger along the windowsill, avoiding his gaze. "You're a man of science, I'm sure you've heard all sorts of zany stories!"

"Have you hit your head recently, Miss Stonewood?" The doctor put his clipboard down and crossed his arms.

"Not that I recall." Annabelle frowned, sensing this was going south.

"Are you under the effects of alcohol?"

"Heavens no! I take it no one has come in here spouting a similar story?" Annabelle asked innocently.

"When did these 'stomach issues' start?" The doctor picked up his clipboard again, ready to take notes.

"My second day on the job. And before you ask me if it's a bout of nerves, I can guarantee you that's not it." She wagged a finger at him. "Us Stonewoods are as cool as cucumbers under stress! This is something else altogether, Doc."

"Have you eaten anything suspicious?" the doctor persisted.

"Unless you call oatmeal or tomato sandwiches suspicious." Annabelle waved her arms in the air in exasperation.

"Fine, we'll perform a full physical examination." The doctor opened the door and called for his receptionist to prep the X-ray machine. "We'll take some X-rays for good measure too."

Somewhat relieved he didn't kick her out, Annabelle did as the doctor said while he checked her temperature, blood pressure, and heart rate. Then he poked and prodded at her stomach, arms, and legs to see if anything was wrong. Still unsatisfied, he sent her over to the X-ray machine.

"Well, I can't see anything that's cause for alarm. But there does appear to be a small circular hole in your hand," the doctor noted curiously as he analyzed the X-ray scans back in his office.

"Oh, that's nothing. Tammy Lynn Carter was jealous I placed before her in the Lil' Southern Miss Pageant a few years back and she stabbed me in the hand with a pen," Annabelle explained as she showed him her hand. "See? All healed!"

"How horribly unnecessary." The doctor shook his head, surprised by this story.

"Pageant queens can be vicious sometimes." Annabelle shrugged. "So doc, is there anything wrong with me?"

"Not according to all the physical tests I've conducted," the doctor sighed, turning a worried gaze on his perplexing patient. "And as far as I know, no stomach issue can alter gravity or impact objects around you ... Perhaps this is more of a *mental* ailment."

"How can it be all in my mind if other people have also witnessed these events with their own eyes?" Annabelle asked earnestly, hurt by this doctor hinting she was crackers when she was only reaching out for help.

"I don't have an answer for you. I know this is not the outcome you were expecting my dear, but I can refer you to a psychologist if you wish," the doctor replied calmly, ready to write the information down on his notepad.

"No, thank you," is all Annabelle could manage to say before storming out of the office and back outside.

She held back tears as she walked to the closest Red Car stop, upset that she thought she would get clear answers for such a bizarre predicament. She knew that doctor did all he could to diagnose her with something, *anything.* But she was still surprised and insulted by the outcome of this unexpected appointment. She had wasted a day away from work and she had nothing to show for it.

Annabelle allowed herself to wallow in self-pity during her journey home, but once she was in the comfort of her room at the boarding house, she set the pity party aside.

"Just because a man of medicine can't find me some answers, it doesn't mean they aren't out there," Annabelle mumbled as she stretched out on her bed. "There are other routes I can take that prove this isn't all in my head."

Chapter 18

"A sick day only one week into the job? That riles me up," Nelson huffed as he paced his office. He basically had over twenty-four hours to work through his frustration about his newest employee not being at work for a day, yet here he was the following morning making her feel lousy about it.

"I wouldn't have done so if I didn't think it was serious, Mr. Beauregard. I even have a doctor's note, see?" Annabelle fetched the crumpled paper out of her purse, but her boss waved it away.

"Everyone has stomach issues from time to time and they don't go running to the doctor! I need employees I can count on," Nelson bellowed, still pacing around the office.

"I can be trusted! I've already made a difference so far, have I not? My expertise has come in handy numerous times!" Annabelle defended herself. She knew her cranky boss was being irrational, but it still made her bristle that he insinuated she was unreliable. She took such criticism to heart.

Nelson stopped pacing, put his hands on his hips and stared at her. "Yeah, I can't argue with that. But I don't want this to become a regular occurrence, you hear?"

"Pos-i-tutely!" Annabelle nodded, relief coursing through her. "Now how can I be of help today?"

"Well, last week was taken over by that accident on the set of *The Enchantress,* so we've fallen behind on some stuff. We have some shorts and features from our B Unit that need to be promoted to the newspapers and magazines. The pitches only need to be a few lines but make it snazzy, we want the public to stick around for the second half of the double bill so we can make more profit." Nelson reached over and grabbed a hefty stack of papers from his desk and plopped them in Annabelle's arms. "Here's a list of the pictures with a brief synopsis of what they're about; it should keep you occupied for most of the day. Now off you go!"

"I'll get started right away," she replied cheerfully. She was about to excuse herself when a random thought blurted out of her mouth. "You know, it's strange to me how everyone keeps referring to Chuck Thorne's death simply as 'an accident'. The word doesn't fully convey the tragedy of it."

"Well, it was an accident after all," he quipped before tilting his head curiously. "What are you driving at anyway? Don't go poking your nose in matters that don't concern you, we stumble upon enough scandals as is!"

"Of course not! I'm just being silly and fretting over nothing." Annabelle added an extra dose of innocent southern twang to disarm the bomb she nearly set off. "Anyhoo, I'll get on these pitches right away!"

She went to her cramped office at the far end of the building. It was basically a converted janitor's closet, and it appeared even smaller when she set the towering stack of papers on her narrow desk. Mr. Beauregard was confining her to this menial task as punishment, but she didn't mind doing grunt work if it paid off in the end. Besides, Annabelle wanted to understand everything the publicity department was involved in, and this was as good a way as any to figure that out.

She zoned in on her task, carefully curating every word of the pitches, and a few hours passed before she knew it. "Boy, some of these pictures sound like real stinkers. Good thing I can spin anything into a more flattering light," she mumbled as she stood up to stretch.

Annabelle's sick day had been more than a little discombobulating and she still felt like a ball of nerves about it. Luckily no other strange episodes had happened since, but she felt like she was walking on eggshells, trying to prevent her own mind from going haywire. On top of that, she felt like her theory about Chuck's possibly intentional death was losing steam. After her conversation with Mrs. Thorne, it was clear she didn't know about the affair so never mind wanting to kill her husband. And that left Annabelle with no other theories. Maybe it was an accident after all.

"Listen, you gotta put this on pause for now." Nelson barged into her office, making Annabelle jump out of her skin and thoughts. "For some reason, Miss Halliwell would like you to join her for a radio program recording."

"Oh." Annabelle was surprised. She was just thinking about the rising star and all of a sudden the dame in question wanted her around!

"Well, why are you still standing there? Don't keep a star waiting, that's the last thing you want to do! Trust me, they get real cranky sometimes, especially Wallace Beery." Nelson's eyes went wide. "But don't ever tell him I said that."

Not having to be told twice, Annabelle made her way across the studio lot to the recording building. She was pointed in the right direction and waited outside the booth as Clover, decked out in a drop-waist dress with strategic billowy fabric details around the midsection, spoke animatedly into a microphone. This building was essential when re-recording bad audio during shooting and often the stars were asked to partake in radio interviews or live recordings of plays and stories. From the looks of it, Clover seemed to be narrating a captivating story.

Annabelle always found it funny when actors could "switch on," becoming almost an entirely new, enigmatic person for the camera. She didn't really get the opportunity to witness it herself when she was an extra. Oftentimes she was in crowded scenes far away from the leads. But with Clover, she could see it and feel it. She saw it during filming on the soundstage, the actress's whole demeanor shifting as she slipped into the role, all the while secretly grieving the death of her lover. And now, even though no cameras were around, Clover was still mesmerizing as she spoke. It was a gift not many people were blessed with, but Annabelle reckoned this star had it.

"Hello, Annabelle. I'm glad you could join the recording." Clover came out of the booth and made a beeline toward her, squeezing her hands amicably. "I hope it wasn't too dull, I've never recorded a radio program before."

"Are you nuts? It was grand, you truly have a knack for this," Annabelle gushed, trying to reign it in a bit. "I'm happy I was here for it."

"Thank you, that's swell" Clover blushed. Contrary to the majority of the established stars, this one didn't come across as a haughty bluenose. Whether all those actors put on an act or not, it got old fast. But it was pretty refreshing to be around a humble actress who was the talk of the town. "I have some free time. Would you like to join me in my dressing room for some sweet tea?"

"That would be the berries! I can never say no to sweet tea," Annabelle exclaimed. She couldn't figure out exactly why Clover wanted her company. Maybe she had some important information to share, or she was just lonely amongst all the hubbub. Annabelle's gut was telling her it was the latter, which she was grateful for because she felt the same way.

They made the trek in Clover's private cart, whipping by all the soundstages and sets until the dressing room apartments materialized in front of them.

"I made this myself at home and I brought some with me. I have a lot of family down south and they always made it when we'd go visit," Clover explained as she went over to her icebox the second they walked into her dressing room. She poured them glasses and handed one over.

"Golly, this takes me back." Annabelle took a sip and closed her eyes. She could almost picture her childhood home with the rickety swing dangling from a tree nearby, the sound of the crickets and wind taking over come sundown. It made her throat constrict for a brief moment.

"I feel like I can fully relax around you," Clover sighed, her hands resting on her belly. "My life is in utter chaos, and I feel like you're the only one who knows and understands."

Annabelle smiled at her. If only she could tell Clover every-thing that was happening to her without seeming bonkers. "I wanted to tell you I paid Mrs. Thorne a visit, claiming I was going on behalf of the publicity department. Don't worry, I didn't mention you and she seemed to be unaware of any affair.

Actually, she talked highly of Chuck *and* you. That might be hard to do when you're in the throes of anger. If she didn't know about it, then it's unlikely she would have wanted him dead."

"Goodness, I'm shocked you had the gumption to go see her." Clover laughed nervously, her face now blotchy. "Did she seem ... upset?"

"Yes, but in a composed way," Annabelle replied. She understood a long time ago to avoid judging people before you knew their full story, and much of the dynamics between these three were not yet known to her. She only wanted to know what was necessary and remain neutral.

Clover nodded, lost in thought. Annabelle looked around the room, giving her host time to process this wallop of information when her eyes settled on a stack of envelopes on a dresser. "Are those letters from your fans? That must be a hoot to read."

Annabelle walked over, picking up the top one. "Gee, whoever wrote this one seems erratic, the penmanship is scribbled and angry. I bet they nearly wrote through the paper!"

"Let me see." Clover snapped back to attention and Annabelle handed over the envelope. She tore it open, scanned it and rolled her eyes. "Not this guy again."

"What is it?" Annabelle couldn't help but be curious.

"This fella seems to be fixated on me, and he sends me anonymous deranged letters professing his love and devotion." Clover waved the letter around. "It's nothing worth fussing over. All the actresses receive them, it comes with the territory unfortunately. You should hear Jean Harlow talk about the letters she receives—that would be a pretty enthralling radio program if you ask me!"

Although part of her wanted to know all the juicy details of the blonde bombshell's fan mail, an alarm went off in Annabelle's gut. "Wait a minute, don't you think your pen pal could be dangerous? Especially in light of your lover falling to his death?"

"I hadn't considered it." Clover blanched suddenly. "Do you think this fella could have found out somehow about my relationship with Chuck and his obsession drove him to murder?"

"Something along those lines ..." Annabelle took the letter from Clover and read it, the words "love" "mine" and "soon" jumping out at her. "I'm thinking either you have one deranged man whose obsession is escalating, or Mrs. Thorne lied to me and she's somehow behind this. It's possible she's a better liar than I thought. Looks like murder is still on the table after all."

"Applesauce," Clover mumbled as she downed her sweet tea. "I don't like my options."

Chapter 19

Feeling both restless and out of sorts the moment she exited the MGM gates, the last thing Annabelle wanted to do was go back to the boarding house and sit in her room. She felt claustrophobic just thinking about it. Instead, she went to the central branch of the Los Angeles Public Library. It would be the perfect place for her to rummage through her disjointed thoughts while not being bothered.

"Gee, this place is bigger than I thought," she mumbled as she walked inside, the high ceilings and rows of bookcases going on forever. Annabelle was a social butterfly by nature, always enjoying being around friends and engaging in lively conversations, but this might be the first time in her life that she wanted peace and quiet. Her parents would be dumbstruck if they knew!

"First things first," she whispered, finding a secluded table away from the checkout counters, grabbing a notepad and pen to jot things down.

She let her thoughts spill out, dedicating a whole page to Chuck Thorne's death and the subsequent information she'd discovered. Clover's name featured prominently, and below it she wrote "Obsessed fan" right next to "Louise Thorne," which she connected with a line and a question mark. Underneath she wrote "Are they one and the same?" It was a whole lot of messy information, and frankly she still wasn't convinced it proved Chuck was pushed off that balcony. She was torn between it being a poorly timed coincidence littered with scandalous loose ends, or a murder of convenience and passion. Either way, she had to do more digging—maybe even have another chat with Louise.

"Like Mama always said, my hard head never gives up," Annabelle huffed, flipping the notepad over to a fresh blank page. Though one of her projects involved solving a murder, this next topic gave her an inordinate amount of the heebie-jeebies.

She didn't even know where to start. Occurrences started happening following that horrendous first day on the set of *The Enchantress* where Chuck Thorne died. These happenings seemed to be linked with her mind and they were escalating in nature, her little earthquake magic trick at the Thorne residence having spooked her enough to seek medical help. Yet there was seemingly no medical condition to diagnose. What on earth was going on?

"Could it be that prop book?" Annabelle tapped the pen on the table, stopping when a nearby patron glared at her.

She had felt a strange sensation when the four women came in contact with it, then the power went out and the following scream bamboozled the rest of the day. It could have been a scene from a picture, really! But was that the starting point? Milagros had seemed more than reluctant to discuss anything relating to that moment when she crossed her path in the wardrobe building, but was she simply skittish by nature? Or was she also experiencing something beyond her control?

To do: find the two other women who touched the prop book, Annabelle wrote, circling the sentence over and over as if it would make the task any easier. The studio employed thousands of people. It would be an absolute pain to track down these dames, but she had to, she had some questions for them. Luckily her new job in the publicity department allowed her to schmooze with most departments on the lot, but she didn't have the luxury of time. She had to contact them before she caused serious damage and suspicion. If only she could better understand what was going on with her body and her mind.

An unpleasant headache started forming right in the centre of Annabelle's forehead and she knew she needed to get up and walk around before it turned into a monstrosity. Growing up, she rarely had the time to enjoy reading. There was always something to do on the farm or she was off doing pageants, but now the stillness of a library made her giddy with possibilities. There was so much knowledge right at her fingertips, and she needed all of it to solve her conundrum.

Annabelle took her time roaming the rows of bookshelves, familiarizing herself with the sections. She snatched up a few books about medicine but found herself browsing the spiritualism and paranormal sections. She grabbed a few of their thick tomes for good measure. With her arms stretched to comical capacity, she went back to her secluded spot and plopped the hefty stack on the table with a loud thud.

"Shh!" an elderly librarian scolded her, holding an icy glare for a beat too long.

"Sorry," Annabelle whispered, not wanting to get booted out

of there when she had so much reading to do.

She sat down cautiously, worried that the creaky chair would send this old lady into a tizzy, and cracked open the first book of her ambitious stack. Annabelle was making up for all those years not spent with her nose in a book, devouring all the information at warp speed while taking incessant notes. She was so engrossed in her research that she didn't notice the sun setting through the windows and all the patrons heading home, making her the only one left hovering under the light of a banker's lamp.

"Young lady, it's time to go. The library is closing." The same old lady came and hovered over Annabelle, snapping her attention back to the present.

"Oh golly! It's late, isn't it?" Annabelle took in her surroundings. Looking down at her chaotic notes, she quickly folded them and shoved them in her purse before the librarian looked too closely. "Let me help you put these books away, I don't want to give you more work at this hour."

"Nonsense dear, it's my job." The librarian started guiding her toward the exit. "Now run along!"

Having been ushered out of the library with the door swiftly locked behind her, Annabelle stood there in a daze. She blinked, her eyes adjusting to the darkness. Her evening's research had opened a whole other world she had never considered before, especially not with her conservative southern upbringing.

She pulled her frenzied notes back out and flipped to the last page where she had circled the word *telekinesis* like a mad woman. All the books about spiritualists and mediums talked about it the same way. When she compared her escalating, unexplained occurrences with this psychic ability, it made more and more sense.

"I'll be damned, but it looks like I've somehow developed the power to move objects with my mind," Annabelle said out loud, letting this insane thought cling to the chilly spring night air. "Now I just need to understand why this happened and how to control it."

Chapter 20

The following morning, Annabelle walked through the MGM gates with one purpose in mind. She followed through with Mr. Beauregard's lowly tasks—evidently, he was still sore with her about the sick day—but after lunch she found an excuse to go visit the wardrobe department.

"Miss Halliwell wants me to have a look at her approved wardrobe both for *The Enchantress* and any forthcoming press events before her extended vacation overseas," Annabelle bluffed. "We've spent quite a bit of time together lately and she trusts my judgement. I wouldn't want to reject her offer and risk having one of our studio's most promising rising stars be on our bad side, now, would we?"

"Of course not, that's the last thing we want!" Nelson barked, rushing her out the door like she was on fire. "Go on then!"

Annabelle chuckled once she was out of earshot. She knew that all she had to do to sway her boss's attention was to pivot the subject and make it sound like it would benefit the publicity department. This trick was already coming in handy.

Just like every time she had to venture across the lot, she looked forward to seeing all the energetic chaos going on around her. Today she spotted dancers practising their steps behind a soundstage for a musical number, a giant wooden replica of a pirate's ship being wheeled around precariously, and two rather well-known actresses squaring off in a shouting match near the edge of the fake Central Park—either real or rehearsed that was up for debate.

"Hello! I'm looking for Milagros? I'm here on behalf of Clover Halliwell," Annabelle asked the wardrobe receptionist, thinking it wise to keep up with her fib for good measure.

"She's out back in the sewing room," the woman replied as she feverishly searched through laundry bags.

Annabelle weaved through the clothes racks and the employees running around with mounds of puffy Civil War-era dresses in their arms until she found the sewing room, the only space in the whole building that seemed relatively quiet despite the machines' whirring. Milagros was the only one in there, hunched over a Singer sewing machine as she ran a delicately detailed navy lace dress through it.

"Why that's a lovely garment! Who is it for?" Annabelle exclaimed after clearing her throat.

Milagros stopped what she was doing and looked up, her face remaining neutral despite the surprise. "It's for Marion Davies's latest picture, another period piece. Mr. Hearst will be stopping by later to approve it, so I need to concentrate."

"Yes naturally." Annabelle was thrown by her bluntness, but it didn't stop her. "I won't take up much of your time. You see, there's been some developments regarding Chuck Thorne's death that make it seem rather suspicious."

"Is that so?" There was a glint in Milagros' brown eyes; she was more than interested.

Annabelle went on to explain what she had uncovered: the

suspicious bruising on the victim's arms which indicated a struggle, Clover Halliwell's romance with the deceased, his widow, and the deranged man who was obsessed with the rising star. The only thing she purposefully left out was the imminent love child.

"And why are you telling me all of this? We are acquaintances at most," Milagros asked, but Annabelle could tell she wasn't recoiling from all this news.

"I had a hunch you'd be intrigued and willing to help," Annabelle replied earnestly. "And us new gals need to stick together! It can be pretty lonely on a big studio lot like this when you don't have any friends."

"Hmm ..." Milagros was pensive as she adjusted her thick braid. "All right, I'll let you know if I come across anything of importance. And don't worry, I can keep it a secret."

"That would be swell, thanks!" Annabelle was relieved and couldn't help but blurt out her findings from the library. "Speaking of secrets, I've been experiencing some bizarre occurrences since that first day on the soundstage. I could only describe it as my mind being able to move objects, and they've been escalating! I thought I was going looney, I mean, how on earth would I be able to do that? I even consulted a doctor who couldn't find anything medically wrong with me, but I didn't give up that easily. I spent hours at the library last night and I think I finally know what's been going on: I now have telekinetic abilities.

"Telekinesis is the ability to move objects with your mind and it all tracks with the little accidents that have been happening around me!" Annabelle continued, nearly breathless. "First it was that water pitcher spilling in my idiot colleague's lap after I had thought of it, then I deviated that scary chunk of wood from falling on Mr. Thalberg and Norma Shearer of all people, and then the worrying 'earthquake' of floating furniture at Mrs. Thorne's home, that was the scariest of all! I've never spent much time contemplating anything related to spiritualism, but there's no denying this is a power I now have. And I think it all started that day."

Milagros had remained mute during this frantic revelation, and it was only once she stopped talking that Annabelle realized it had been the wrong move.

"I realize how kooky I sound, but it all started after that first day of filming on *The Enchantress* and something tells me it has something to do with that prop book we touched. Have you been experiencing ... anything out of the ordinary as well?"

"I need to get back to work," was all Milagros said before turning her attention back to her sewing machine, having officially retreated within, now ignoring this strange woman spouting nonsense.

Annabelle stood there dumbfounded; she had messed up this conversation and didn't know how to turn it around. This was the first time she was in such a predicament. She was normally great at using her personality and conversation skills to wiggle out of uncomfortable situations, but this time she was left stunned.

"Miss Stonewood, there's an urgent call for you back at the publicity building." The receptionist popped her head into the room before running off.

"Urgent?" Annabelle turned to Milagros one last time before leaving. "Well, you know where to find me if you ever want to talk."

As she power walked back to her department, Annabelle cursed under her breath. How could she have derailed that conversation so badly? Milagros had been receptive to the Chuck mystery, why couldn't she have just left it at that? But no, she had to open her big mouth about her telekinesis theory, losing all credibility in the wardrobe assistant's eyes.

"I should have clued into her complete shyness and not pushed so much on her. I know better than that," Annabelle huffed, but she knew she needed to share this whopper of a secret with someone. Clover was already going through too much, she couldn't put that extra burden on her. Besides, she was under the impression Milagros knew more than she was letting on about the prop book.

"Hopefully she won't be utterly frightened by me. I do hope we get the chance to talk again," Annabelle mumbled as she let herself into the publicity building.

"Hiya! You can take the call in your office," Ginny explained as Annabelle walked by her desk.

"Perfect, thank you." Annabelle's worry grew a little more. Was it a call from Texas? Were her parents sick?

She quietly closed her office door and picked up the telephone receiver on her desk, expecting to hear the voice of a relative. But she was thrown for a loop once again. "Hello, Annabelle speaking ... Mrs. Thorne calm down, what's wrong?"

Chapter 21

"Sorry to keep you waiting, my boss would have had a fit if I even considered leaving early," Annabelle explained as she approached a defeated-looking Louise Thorne. "Have you been sitting here since you called me?"

"I suppose so." Louise's eyes were glassy and unfocused.

Annabelle had raced to the Red Car the moment she clocked out and met the new widow on a park bench outside a Security First National Bank. Her hands were oddly empty considering the frantic call where she blubbered about finding something horrifying.

"Where are the letters?" Annabelle asked, hoping they hadn't been torn up in fury. That would be a lousy way to lose evidence.

"In the bank. They wouldn't let me leave with them," Mrs. Thorne replied, getting up and motioning Annabelle to follow her.

They walked back into the silent bank where the clacking of their heels on the marble floor rang unusually loud as they walked all the way to the back of the building where an employee was standing guard over a locked door.

"She's with me, I need to see the contents of my late husband's lock box again," Louise said.

"Certainly." The bank employee gave a slight nod as he let

them in. They went into a garishly bright room where the walls comprised lock boxes from floor to ceiling. He jangled a hefty set of keys, retrieved the correct box, and left it open on a metal table at the centre of the room. "I'll give you some privacy."

They waited for the employee to close the door behind him before looking at each other, then the box, and each other again. The room felt airless and cold. After an unnatural throat clearing sound, Louise gestured for Annabelle to take a peek.

Annabelle had never used a lock box before and had no idea what to expect. What did people even keep in these things? Mundane documents like insurance papers, contracts, jewelry, family photographs? Or would someone hide something away from their significant other? It turns out she was right on the money with her theory of a hidden secret.

She took a stack of letters out of the box and for a second she thought, *Jeepers, I hope these aren't sappy love letters between Chuck and Clover! How horrendous that would be.* They were personal letters all right, but they were the opposite of lovey-dovey.

"He was being blackmailed," Annabelle gasped, eyes still glued on the papers. "And for a while according to these."

"Chuck never uttered a word about this." Louise shook her head and crossed her arms. "And an affair, too!"

"Jiminy Christmas," Annabelle mumbled as she skimmed through the letters more rapidly. The other party wasn't named in these letters, so Clover was in the clear for now—doubly so on the pregnancy front. "This is a lot of information to process. What do you think of all this?"

"I feel sad, betrayed, and angry!" Louise huffed, much less composed than during their first conversation. "He put himself in a scandalous situation and some monster was trying to extort money out of it. How abominable!"

"Do you have an inkling of who he'd be having an affair with?" Annabelle asked, finally looking up from the letters. She desperately didn't want to get the jitters and cause all these lock boxes to fly out of the walls.

"No one is coming to mind," Louise sighed. "Communication was not our strong suit, we lived on different planets most of the time. But that part is the least of my worries! I have a bone-deep feeling that Chuck's death is linked to this threatening blackmailer and that it wasn't an accident after all. You were there that day, what do you think?"

"After the fall happened and police were roaming around, I did notice some rather intense bruising appear on your husband's arms. It looked consistent with a fresh struggle to my untrained eye, but no one would hear anything of it." Annabelle felt relieved that she could finally come clean about her initial suspicion, what had started her down this path. "I'm terribly sorry I didn't bring it up when we first met. The whole world was so adamant it was an accident, and I didn't have anything else to go on! I felt like a silly girl with a wild imagination."

"I understand." Louise gave her a weak smile, then her ears turned red with fury. "But now we sure do! I know we had our problems and he certainly played with fire, but Chuck was a swell man, and he didn't deserve to be met with such a horrifying end."

Annabelle hated to do this, but it was necessary. "Excuse me for a moment I need to ask our friend a quick question."

She left the room, found the familiar employee by the water

cooler, and inadvertently startled him.

"Good heavens! Is everything all right with Mrs. Thorne? We were terribly sorry to hear about Mr. Thorne's sudden death," he said as he smoothed his tie.

"Yes, it's quite tragic." Annabelle lowered her voice before asking, "Listen, was Mr. Thorne the only one who ever used this lock box? Had Mrs. Thorne ever come in here to use it?"

"No, it was just him. We take these things seriously, we even make customers sign contracts," the employee explained. "He was the only one with a key and he was the only person allowed near the box until today unfortunately. Naturally, the bank has a master key in case of emergencies, but we use a logbook and a buddy system. No one tried accessing it with the master key either, I double checked myself."

"I see. Thank you for your thorough explanation, I needed that for clarification." Annabelle smiled and turned on her heels, making her way back to the lock box and Mrs. Thorne.

"Where the devil did you go?" Louise asked incredulously.

"I needed to confirm who had access to this box and if it had been tampered with somehow," Annabelle explained, keeping her tone neutral. She was relieved Louise was no longer a suspect, and from the looks of it, the widow didn't have a clue she had been considered one to begin with.

"So where do we go from here? Is there anything you could check out at the studio?" Louise asked with a hint of desperation. "It happened on a soundstage after all, someone must know something!"

"I think I know of a good place to start." Annabelle scanned through the letters again. Some were typed up with a typewriter, but others were written in ink, and they reminded her of

Clover's deranged fan letters. There could be more than one maniac who loved to correspond with letters, but once again that would be a big coincidence considering Clover and Chuck were a serious item. "I need to take one of these, one written with a fountain pen. I have a hunch, and I need to do some snooping to confirm it."

"All right, but please keep me updated." Louise seemed exhausted, no amount of perfect hair or makeup could disguise it today.

"What are you going to do with this information?" Annabelle asked, tucking the one letter into her purse.

"If the police were so quick to rule it an accident, I doubt they'll reopen the case now." Louise rubbed her temples. "And I don't want Chuck's indiscretions to be known publicly. I'd like to keep this between us until we have enough to cause a fuss."

"Sounds good to me," Annabelle said as they closed the lock box and put it back in its slot.

They said their goodbyes outside and went their separate ways. Annabelle was eager to get home to write down all these developments. Louise was no longer on the list of suspects but there was now a blackmailer as well as a deranged fan—what a doozy! Annabelle would bet some kale that they were one and the same, but that still wouldn't simplify the mystery.

On top of all that, she was now the keeper of secrets for both Clover *and* Louise. She'd have to pay extra close attention to what information she divulged, this wasn't the time to get into more hot water. Plus, she had secrets of her own to contend with—some pretty active ones at that!

"And I thought the publicity department would be a handful,"

Annabelle grunted as she ran to catch up with the Red Car.

Chapter 22

Having found another fictional reason to go tend to Clover, this time settling on the obscure term of "feminine problems," Mr. Beauregard once again gave Annabelle permission to go see the rising star. She felt like a laser-focused bull in a china shop, trying to weave her way across the lot, everything conveniently getting in her way. The path was always relatively clear when she had all the time in the world, but all human or object barriers appeared in front of her when she needed to step to it.

Annabelle ran up the stairs of the actresses' apartments, not caring about her frazzled appearance for once. She stomped down the balcony, Clover's apartment in sight, when another famous face made a surprising exit from her own room, Annabelle nearly colliding with her face-on.

"My apologies, Miss Garbo!" Annabelle gasped, feeling mortified. She didn't want to be the reason this excruciatingly reclusive actress remained indoors for good. "I should be paying more attention to where I'm going."

Greta Garbo simply sized her up and gave her a neutral shrug before walking around her and going down the stairs, leaving Annabelle befuddled. She truly was a perplexing woman. Annabelle shook this odd encounter off her shoulders, loudly knocked three times on Clover's door, and let herself in.

"There's been a startling development," Annabelle announced sternly as she entered the room. "Someone knew about your dalliance and was blackmailing Chuck about it."

"Horsefeathers! And next time don't barge in here spouting confidential information like that, I could have had company," Clover chastised her, turning to the side in her makeup chair as she tightly gripped the armrests. "So, you're saying someone out there knows about Chuck and me? What about the ..."

"There was no mention of the pregnancy in the blackmail letters. We're still in the clear on that front," Annabelle explained as she sat down on the couch, suddenly winded from her frantic excursion over here.

"Where did you even find these letters?" Clover asked, prying herself away from the chair to pour herself a glass of water with shaky hands.

"They were in a secret lock box Chuck kept at the bank. Louise found the key hidden away in a drawer," Annabelle explained, looking away.

"How awful," Clover's eyes darted wildly. "Does she know I'm the other woman?"

"She doesn't have a clue and frankly she wasn't too torn up about it. What disturbed her more was knowing a threatening person was in her late husband's life. She certainly thinks there's foul play now, those letters are pretty damning."

"Jeepers that's right." Clover exhaled sharply. "That fall doesn't seem so accidental now when there's a blackmailer in the picture."

"I also think this predator could be behind another set of letters." Annabelle cocked an eyebrow.

"Do you mean my fan who sends me those unsettling love letters?" Clover's eyes widened; she clearly hadn't considered the link until now.

"Mm-hmm." Annabelle nodded, pulling out the evidence she took from the lock box. "This fella used a typewriter for most of his missives, but a few were handwritten. I was thinking I could compare them with your fan letters. I take it you've tossed out the previous ones, but what if I go to the fan mail department and pick up your letters for the day? If he's as consistent as you say he is, they'll be another in there waiting to be read."

"Sure, let me write you a little note saying I give you approval to pick up my letters." Clover grabbed a notepad and pen from an end table, scribbled something quickly and handed it to Annabelle. "They can get pretty tough on people, wanting to make sure stuff doesn't get in the wrong hands. Now I think I'll indulge in a mid-morning nap. Both me and the baby need to process the bombshell you let off in here."

Closing the door quietly behind her as Clover stretched out on the couch, Annabelle once again scurried off like a mouse with a cat on its tail. This rising star sure was dealt some bad luck lately. The married father of your secret unborn baby is possibly murdered on the set of what is already being dubbed your biggest hit? She must be beyond her wits' end. Hopefully Annabelle's latest hunch will bring them one step closer to finding the culprit.

Annabelle walked into the fan mail department and was met by utter chaos. There was a long counter dividing the fan mail employees from their fellow MGM colleagues who came to collect mail, and people were hooting and hollering on both sides. There was a glass partition behind the employees and beyond was a sea of mail being organized and sorted into rows of bins.

"Golly, this is a whole different kind of rodeo," Annabelle mumbled as she worked the courage to elbow her way to the counter, brandishing Clover's note in one hand. "Hi! I'm here to pick up Miss Halliwell's fan mail."

"I've never seen you before!" a short man bellowed as he clomped on over, snatching the note from her hand and grunting audibly. "Fine. Wait here."

Annabelle stared mindlessly in front of her, her mind going slack with the high volume of voices around her, until some key words caught her attention.

"I'm here to pick up Miss Harlow's mail, please," a woman behind Annabelle's back announced. "I'm her assistant, Velma French."

"Oh wow, you're Jean Harlow's assistant! She seems like such a swell—" Annabelle started as she pivoted around to face this woman, only to realize she had seen her before. It was one of the other dames who had touched that darn prop book at the same time as Milagros and herself. "Say, weren't you on the soundstage of *The Enchantress* the day that lighting technician fell? I think we both bent down to pick up a prop when the place went dark."

"What about it?" The fellow assistant turned and glared at her, her short black bob as sharp as her cheekbones.

"Did you happen to see anything strange before the accident?" Annabelle wasn't expecting such a frosty reception, but she soldiered on. "I don't recall you being interrogated by the coppers."

"I hightailed it out of there the moment the lights switched back on." Velma continued to glare at Annabelle. "Miss Harlow wanted me to hand deliver a letter to Clover, that's the only reason I was allowed on that soundstage. And I hadn't paid much mind to the balcony, that's not my department."

"I see." Annabelle tried collecting her thoughts as a hefty bag of Harlow's fan letters were handed over to Velma. This tomato wasn't pleased to be talking about that fateful day, but she still had to ask. "One last thing before you go. Has anything strange happened to you since that day, particularly after touching that book? Objects moving unnaturally or anything like that?"

"What did you say your name was?" Velma asked suspiciously, that sour look not leaving her face.

"Annabelle Stonewood. I'm a new publicity assistant," she replied eagerly.

"Well Annabelle, I recommend you only spin stories for the fan magazines, and leave your fellow employees alone." With that, Velma flung the mail bag over her shoulder in one swift motion, nearly grazing Annabelle's face in the process, and left the building.

"I sure hope she doesn't talk to Jean Harlow that way," Annabelle scoffed, the sting of rejection making her cheeks go red.

Chapter 23

"It sure looks like I'll be pulling an all-nighter," Annabelle sighed, taking a sip of bitter coffee as she stared at all of Clover Halliwell's latest fan mail dumped on her bedroom floor. Back in her pageant days, Annabelle thought she was the bee's knees for receiving a handful of letters from admiring locals, but this stack really put her to shame. She bet the top stars like Joan Crawford and Norma Shearer had their assistants handling this full-time; there was no way they could reply to all of these themselves!

Annabelle sat cross-legged on the creaky floor, trying to determine if she should come up with a system for sorting these. "Let's keep it simple and have a pile for suspicious letters and another for the ones that seem on the level."

With the help of a trusty letter opener, Annabelle opened envelopes one after another and read through each letter diligently, not wanting to overlook any detail. This went on for hours under the light of a few strategically placed lamps. The majority of the fans wrote in with cute and mundane requests.

"Would you please enclose your signature for my collection?"

"I would love to hear about your typical day on set. It must be magical."

"What are the Barrymores really like? I'm dying to know!"

Most of them were quite touching for their sincerity, and others were a laugh.Why people felt the need to spout off their opinions about trivial things like what Miss Halliwell ate for breakfast was beyond Annabelle's comprehension. But so far, there was no letter from the blackmailer or anything else concerning.

"Oh brother, my poor legs!" Annabelle stood up cautiously, her one foot completely asleep. After a few painful shakes, she went and stood by her window, opening it a crack to get some fresh air.

She couldn't say her first trip to the fan mail department was a pleasant one—the employees in there seemed so cranky! Although Miss Velma French took the title of crankiest of them all. It went against Annabelle's every instinct to be rude with someone right off the bat, yet that's exactly what Velma greeted her with the moment she opened her mouth. Usually, she could brush it off, but she couldn't do that when she needed information from this dame, and judging from her standoffish behaviour, she was clearly keeping something under wraps.

"Other than befriending Clover, my ability to make friends in Tinseltown hasn't been stellar," Annabelle mused. "I'm usually good at it!"

There hadn't been a telekinetic moment since her first encounter with Louise Thorne, but she constantly felt like a ticking time bomb about to fling furniture and various objects left and right. But what if her interpretation of its origin was off? What if it was purely a fluke that these abilities started after that first day on the soundstage? There's a possibility there was no correlation with that prop book and those other ladies. It would certainly explain why both Milagros and Velma bristled at her questions, thinking she was absolutely mad and questioning the publicity department for hiring her. Annabelle couldn't deny there was a slight chance that whatever was going on only had to do with her mind and body. But still, she couldn't help but wonder, and her hard head couldn't let it go.

"That's enough of that." She clapped her hands for no one's benefit other than her own. "There's still a hefty pile of letters to sort through."

She resumed her position on the floor and got back to work. It was only after another two hours passed, accompanied with a caffeine refill, that Annabelle stumbled upon another deranged note from Clover's so-called "biggest admirer." She reached over and took the lock box letter out of her purse, smoothing both out side by side on the floor.

"Well, I'll be damned. They're one and the same!" Annabelle leaned in closer. Not only was the scratchy writing mirroring itself to the letter, but so was the aggressive language and turns of phrase. There was no denying this lunatic was overly captivated by Clover and intent on making Chuck pay, presumably both literally and figuratively, for his indiscretions with the focus of his obsession.

She'd had an inkling they were the same person but now she had some satisfying proof on paper. But now what? It made a solid piece of evidence for murder, but they needed more to build an actual case. She would have to have more in-depth conversations with both Clover and Louise to try and narrow down a common denominator other than the murder victim and take it from there.

"I might as well read the rest of these." Annabelle eyed the remaining unopened letters. "Maybe this delinquent wrote more—he is crazy enough to not stop at one."

Her discovery had left her feeling a little uplifted, her suspicions having been confirmed. But this last batch of letters quickly made that feeling vanish out the window.

"What the devil is this?" Annabelle exclaimed loudly, juggling three letters in her hands, and reading an excerpt out loud.

"*I loved our night together, my darling, the restaurant you chose was sublime. I'm hoping you will grant me the honour of taking you out again sometime, maybe to the Cocoanut Grove ... am I imagining things?*"

All three letters in her hand were signed with three different names and expressed the same sentiment: having gone on a date with Clover and wanting to take her out again. There were enough details in there to make Annabelle believe these encounters were legitimate and not make-believe, but why hadn't Clover mentioned them before? Was it possible she had more beaux than just Chuck Thorne?

"Oh applesauce, this sure complicates everything!" Annabelle whined, tossing the letters on the floor. It was already tense enough with a deranged fan-blackmailer but now there were more men vying for Miss Halliwell's affections? That multiplied their suspects list and Annabelle was sour about it. She thought she was slowly getting somewhere but now it felt like someone had let a bag of marbles loose on the floor for her to slip up. "Boy does Clover have some explaining to do."

Chapter 24

"Miss Stonewood! Come in my office," Nelson barked the second Annabelle set foot in the publicity building.

"Sure thing, Mr. Beauregard." Annabelle looked at Ginny, mouthed *what's gotten into him?* but only got an apologetic shrug in response.

She walked into her boss's office and her colleague Cooper Mason, the only one who seemed close to her in age, was also in there. Going by the look on his face, he had also been summoned harshly.

"I have a special task for both of you today." Nelson cleared his throat, holding a stack of papers in his hands. "We've organized a publicity stunt to help promote our upcoming B-movies. We don't have any trouble with the ones with big name celebrities, but these need an extra push. We have a float going around Los Angeles today—you don't need to worry about the route, it's already been taken care of. Some of the actors in these B-movies will be sitting on the float along with Percival, and all I need you to do is follow behind and hand out pamphlets to any passersby."

"Who's Percival?" Annabelle asked. She didn't remember creating a star persona for someone with that name.

"You don't know who Percival is?" both Nelson and Cooper

said in unison.

"I'm not from here, remember?" Annabelle responded in an innocent sing-song voice.

"Percival the panda of course! He'll be sat in the centre of the float and a banner will read 'MGM brings you the exotic every day' written on the side. It's genius." Nelson seemed pretty proud of himself. He split the stack of pamphlets in two and handed it to them. "Since you two are my rookies, these types of stunts get assigned to you. Now off you go, you have a big day ahead of you!"

"Golly, a publicity stunt with a panda? That's quite different," Annabelle giggled as the two rookies exited the building. "Have you handled these events before?"

"Yeah, once it was with a pack of lion cubs, but it got unruly pretty quickly. Someone got a small part of their ear bitten off," Cooper replied. "You'll get used to the antics with time."

They walked over to one of MGM's side entrances where the promotional float was already set up with Percival sitting comfortably in the middle, completely unfazed by all the hoopla. To Annabelle's surprise, there was a small marching band and a few chorus girls paying close attention as one of the studio's directors explained the path they were about to take and the routine that would match each street. This fella wasn't high up on the director's totem pole, but he took this job very seriously.

"All right, places everyone! It's show time!" he bellowed as the gates lurched open and he took his spot on the small ledge at the back of the float.

"Okay kid, the main thing we gotta do is walk behind the float, smile big, and hand out these pamphlets to folks. It sounds simple, but you'll be dying to sit down after a full day of this."

"I'm not worried, I'm used to being on my feet and entertaining a crowd," she replied, excited to perform publicity duties off the lot.

The band played loudly, and the float moved slowly, with Percival lazily eating bamboo sticks as passersby watched on in amusement. Annabelle had attended parades before, but this felt different. Usually, people knew about a parade ahead of time and were already gathered on the sidewalk in anticipation. Although this publicity stunt already had a designated route blocked off, all the people they crossed didn't know what was going on, meaning the MGM performers and employees had to exude extra energy to entice citizens to stand by for the show. Luckily Percival the panda helped with catching attention. How many pandas did you see roaming about Culver City?

After four hours of exaggerated pep and pamphlets being handed out, the float and crew stopped off on a side road in Hollywood, eager to rest their feet and to hydrate.

"Great job, everybody!" The director clapped to get everyone's attention. "Now I bet everyone is ready to have some lunch. We pulled some strings and the Brown Derby around the corner is waiting for us. Have some cobb salad and soda courtesy of MGM!"

The director had barely finished his sentence before a small stampede had scurried off, salivating. It was nice and cool in the restaurant which was needed after the hot spring sun beat down on their heads all morning. The crew of the publicity stunt ate up in silence as Percival's handler set up some parasols around his prized possession and misted the panda with water.

"Gee, that big guy is getting the star treatment," Annabelle giggled as she looked out the window, sipping on her Coca-Cola bottle. "He'll develop an ego pretty soon."

"I bet he already has one, he keeps giving me the stink eye!" Cooper guffawed, sitting across from Annabelle in a booth.

She hadn't spent much one-on-one time with her male colleagues and talking to Cooper was surprisingly pleasant. It was just a shame that they all felt the need to look down and belittle her while all together. But it was all water off a duck's back to Annabelle; it just showed how insecure men could be around smart women.

"Say, you've been spending quite a bit of time with Clover Halliwell since day one of shooting *The Enchantress*. How's she holding up? There sure is a lot of pressure on her right now, all the papers are saying this picture is her big moment," Cooper added before taking a healthy bite of his cold cut sandwich.

"Oh, you know, she doesn't have her own assistant and Mr. Beauregard thought it would be a good test for me as his newest employee." Annabelle shrugged, trying to appear nonchalant when she had been dying to chat with Clover since she found three new beaux in her mail. "It's been tough since that lighting technician fell but I think she'd holding up."

"I thought I saw you leave the fan mail department yesterday. That building sure is a zoo!" Cooper smirked.

"I offered to help Clover with her mail on my personal time and I gotta say I wasn't expecting that many letters." Annabelle shook her head in disbelief. "Many men are infatuated with her, I can tell you that much."

"Who wouldn't be?" Cooper gulped down the rest of his soda. "She's a looker and she's a swell actress—that's an irresistible combination."

"Yeah, and it's attracted at least one fella who doesn't have his head screwed on just right." Annabelle was curious to know if her colleague knew something worthwhile, but she had to be careful not to reveal too much. "She says all the actresses receive letters like that every once in a while, but this one seems pretty persistent! Has the publicity department dealt with anything like this before?"

"Not particularly. Unless someone tried doing a big grand gesture that we could capitalize on, it's none of our business," Cooper replied. "But you know, all the starlets try to take shortcuts to get to the top and that could ruffle some feathers. Many of them date multiple men at once, using them as meal tickets and such.But they need to realize there are consequences to their actions. That's how it works around here. Maybe Miss Halliwell is no different than the rest of them."

"Is that so?" Annabelle pinched her wrist under the table, resisting the urge to roll her eyes. It was so matter-of-fact to him. "I'd like to think women's dating lives shouldn't be scrutinized any more than the men's romantic endeavours. If actors can rely on their talents, then so can actresses."

"Sure, whatever you say," Cooper laughed dismissively.

"All right folks, we still have another four hours of promoting ahead of us," the director bellowed near the front door, saving Annabelle from this dead-end conversation. "We're walking all the way down to Santa Monica so let's give everyone a grand show, shall we?"

The small crew groaned as they got back to their feet, thanked the manager of the Brown Derby, and ventured back out into the sun. Annabelle resumed her position behind the float, plastering on a peppy smile as their procession started up again.

This day reminded her of a travelling circus. Not only because of this extravagant stunt they were performing, but also because women basically lived on a Ferris wheel controlled by men. They lived in a bubble and only moved in one direction, risking falling off if they no longer wanted to go on this circular journey that wasn't to their advantage.

Annabelle's disappointing conversation with Cooper proved what she assumed most men, on set and off, felt about actresses and their dalliances or lack thereof. If it benefitted a fella, all the power to him. But if it didn't, there'd be never-ending judgement and hell to pay. With that logic, that deranged fan of Clover's could be *any man* and that terrified Annabelle. Sure, she was somewhat irritated that her new confidante had kept a few extra beaux under wraps, but maybe their male delusions could lead the way to a breakthrough. That's what she kept telling herself anyway.

"This might be the most unpleasant conversation yet, but Clover has to come clean," Annabelle mumbled through gritted teeth before handing off pamphlets to a crowd of eager onlookers.

Chapter 25

Her feet still sore from following a panda float around Los Angeles for eight hours the day before, Annabelle was a little cranky despite her best outward efforts at disguising it. Neither Cooper nor she had received any comment or thanks from their boss for their gruelling legwork. Instead, they were greeted with a new set of menial tasks. She couldn't speak to her colleague's work ethic since that promotional stunt was their first time working closely together, but she certainly proved her worth enough to avoid this wishy-washy attitude from her boss.

"One day I'm assigned to host gossip columnist around the lot, and the next I'm filing mountains of press clippings away," Annabelle sighed, hunched over a drawer of file folders in the filing room.

With lunch break approaching like a saving grace, Annabelle walked over to the commissary like a zombie, settling on chicken pot pie and iced tea before trying to find a place to sit. She spotted a cluster of extras she had worked with in the past but decided to find a quiet spot instead. She had worked in competitive environments before, but she'd rather avoid the cattiness and hushed conversations if she could. You could do well for yourself and move on up without having to rely on bamboozling your competition's reputation. Her mother always said kindness makes the world go round.

Despite the physical exhaustion that dragged her down, she felt jittery. She needed to find Clover and sort this beaux business out before this turned into the script of a melodrama the screenplay department would churn out.

After finishing her lunch, Annabelle ventured over to Miss Halliwell's dressing room and knocked three times but got no response.

"Darn it, she must be on the soundstage." Annabelle glanced at her watch. She had just enough time to walk by the set while heading back to the publicity department before her break was up. She couldn't just wait around outside her dressing room; Miss Garbo would surely call security on her and that wouldn't do her any good.

She picked up the pace, eliciting some funny looks as she strode on by. Lucky for her, she found Clover getting some air next to the soundstage in the shade.

"Ah, Annabelle, what a pleasant surprise!" Clover laughed nervously. It's like she knew what to expect. She clutched the black shawl, which was part of her bewitching costume, closer around her body. "So are my fan and the blackmailer one and the same?"

"Yes, they are, but you're right on the money with the word *surprise* because that revelation wasn't the last of it!" Annabelle quipped. She wanted to keep her tone neutral, but she couldn't help feeling duped that Clover had only told her half the truth about her love life.

"I take it you're not pleased with what you found in my fan

mail?" Clover smiled sheepishly.

"And how!" Annabelle put her hands on her hips just like when her own mother scolded her for sass mouthing. She noticed a lot of crew members roaming about and cocked her head. "Let's go for a walk so we can talk in private."

"All right, but they want me back inside in ten minutes," Clover added as she followed Annabelle across to a fake old western town and sat on the steps of a weathered saloon.

"I'd like to start off by saying that I'm not sore because you've had multiple secret beaux. I'm frazzled because it's important since I'm helping you *solve a murder*. We can't count anyone out and spurned romantic interests are often at the top of the suspects list!" Annabelle explained through gritted teeth.

"I know. Golly, I feel silly." Clover covered her face with her hands, trying to prevent an onset of tears, which had been happening a lot considering her predicament. "I cut them out of my life the moment I found out I was pregnant. I always tossed any letters from them so it hadn't occurred to me that I should mention them ... I'm dreadfully sorry Annabelle. I don't want you to think I was keeping anything from you."

"Is there even the slightest chance any of them could be the father or even know about this secret?" Annabelle asked bluntly. "Once again, I'm only asking this for the sake of our investigation."

"Heavens no! Chuck was the only one I was intimate with," Clover replied, guard up. "And if the others had an inkling about it, they would have gone to the press by now. I'm sure they'd get a hefty sum for a scoop on Clover Halliwell."

"Hmm, I see what you're driving at." Annabelle nodded. "So, I found letters from three fellas. Tell me about them and spare no details, it's important."

"There's not much to tell! I was lonely and looking for ways to pass the time." Clover shrugged. "I met Brick while running errands and we went out to the beach a few times but he's a travelling salesman and he's out of town more often than not. To be quite frank, I got the impression I was one of many gals he was courting. And I bumped into Perry at the Santa Monica Pier, and we hit it off initially. But he owned a few White Castles around Los Angeles, and it became apparent he was more smitten by those burgers than any dame, even though his ego wouldn't admit it. Despite them sending me letters here and there, I'm confident neither Brick nor Perry would give a hoot enough about me to break into the lot and cause trouble, especially if they weren't aware of that trouble to begin with."

"Fair enough," Annabelle sighed. "And what about the third one?"

"Nathaniel Stanley? He's an extra here at MGM," Clover started. "We would have lunch together in the commissary and we went to see pictures a few times. I recall him not being too pleased I didn't want to go on dates with him anymore. Plus, he seemed miffed that I started making a name for myself while he was still relegated to the shadows."

"Sounds like jealousy to me. Have you ever witnessed him being mean?" Annabelle asked.

"Well, he was awfully rude to wait staff when we'd go out. It would make me feel uncomfortable, but I hadn't thought much of it until now and I haven't crossed him around the lot in a long time." Clover frowned. "Do you think he could be heartless enough to commit murder?"

"Let's see, he's infatuated with you and he's jealous of your rising fame." Annabelle counted off on her fingers. "If he somehow found out about your affair with a member of the crew, that could have sent him over the edge. He could be moonlighting as an anonymous deranged fan to keep the heat off him, that's also a possibility. Plus, he could have easily walked onto the soundstage unnoticed. He's an extra after all, they blend in."

"Oh brother." Clover took a deep inhale. "It all adds up, doesn't it?"

"Miss Halliwell, we need you on set!" a production assistant yelled from across the way.

"You go ahead and get back to work," Annabelle reassured the frazzled actress. "I'll try to coordinate an accidental meeting with Nathaniel."

Chapter 26

"Hi Ginny, do you mind making this call for me? It'll sound more official if it comes from the receptionist," Annabelle asked as she slid a paper toward her. "Here's what I want you to say."

"Sure," Ginny said with a shrug. "As long as you're not trying to get me in trouble!"

"Of course not!" Annabelle waved and smiled innocently. "I wouldn't do such a thing."

After Clover fessed up to going on a few dates with fellow MGM employee Nathaniel Stanley, Annabelle had tried her best to do some discreet snooping about this jealous bit player. Slipping back into "pageant queen mingling mode," she mentioned him in conversation with her colleagues and even with some employees she accosted in the commissary. Luckily, her previous position as an extra herself who was now a publicity assistant made her questions appear rather mundane, which worked in her favour. She had managed to narrow down what movie set he could be working on, but she needed an official confirmation before waltzing on over there.

"Yes, I'm calling from the publicity department." Ginny cleared her throat, gripping the receiver in one hand as she glanced at Annabelle's paper. "Mr. Beauregard has taken a particular interest in this production and would like to know which extras you currently have on set ... He's forming a plan to groom some of them to move on up. You know how things move fast around here ... Yes exactly, I need you to read the list of them back to me ... Hey, I don't call the shots around here, I'm only the receptionist! I'm simply following Mr. Beauregard's instructions and I suggest you do the same.He is a close friend of Mr. Mayer, after all."

Annabelle stood by and smirked at the exchange. Ginny seemed willing to go along with anything despite her innocent yet misleading calm exterior. She took note of it; not only was this a good quality for a potential friend but it would be useful in a business sense as well.

"Uh-huh ..." Ginny tapped a pen on her desk as she listened to someone rattle off names on the other end. "All right, I will let Mr. Beauregard know. Thank you."

"And?" Annabelle asked impatiently as Ginny put the telephone receiver back on its hook. "Is Nathaniel Stanley on set right now?"

"He sure is." Ginny nodded. "On the soundstage for the filming of *Speak Easily*. I gotta say, being an extra on the set of a Buster Keaton and Thelma Todd picture must be a hoot. They don't have an unfunny bone in their bodies!"

"I'll say! Thanks for all your help, Ginny, you're the berries." Annabelle gave her a wink and dashed out the building.

Despite her outward confidence, this task left Annabelle a little jittery. Not only did she have to sneak into a soundstage, but she also had to approach this Stanley fella the right way if she wanted to get viable information out of him. She halted in front of Stage 21 which was only one row over from where Clover was filming *The Enchantress*. The red light wasn't flashing, meaning the cameras weren't rolling.

"Well, here goes nothing." Annabelle fluffed her blonde curls, took a deep breath, and opened the door.

To her surprise, no one was monitoring the entrance. Instead, all the cast and crew were congregated near a specific set farther in; all the cameras and lights pointing at it.

"Aaaannd ACTION!" a portly male director yelled from his chair.

Annabelle approached cautiously, making sure to not trip or bump into anything that could ruin the take and draw attention to herself. She could talk her way out of a jam, but that hypothetical blunder would surely get back to Mr. Beauregard and she did not want to be in hot water with him—especially when she was getting to the bottom of a crime.

As she tiptoed closer, she watched a slapstick scene unfold between Buster and Thelma and she was mesmerized by their comedic chops. You really needed the right instincts to pull it off. It was only after the director yelled again that she snapped out of her reverie.

"CUT! All right let's take five folks, we need to set up for the next scene," he yelled from the comfort of his chair.

The cast and crew dispersed and it was with horror that Annabelle realized she hadn't the faintest idea what Nathaniel Stanley looked like. Clover had discussed his personality at length but there were no physical details to help her single him out.

"Rats," Annabelle hissed, looking around to find some sort of lowly production assistant she could bother. She spotted an insecure-looking young man with thick glasses and she approached him. "Hello, I'm Miss Stonewood from the publicity department and I need to speak with Mr. Nathaniel Stanley, he's an extra."

"Now?" the young man stuttered. "We're filming!"

"It will only take two minutes, I promise." she squeezed his arm and that did the trick.

"Nathaniel Stanley! Nathaniel Stanley! Publicity needs to speak with you." The young man raised his fluctuating voice.

Annabelle stood close by until an attractive man with chiseled features and wavy dark hair approached. She could see why Clover would entertain a few dates with this fella.

"I'm Nathaniel, what seems to be the problem?" he asked, looking from the production assistant to Annabelle, his demeanor getting a smidge flirtier when he looked her up and down.

"Hello Mr. Stanley, Mr. Beauregard sent me over and I have a few questions for you. Can we step outside for a minute?" Annabelle asked, already walking toward the exit.

"Sure, anything for a pretty dame." Nathaniel winked as he followed her out into the sun.

She led him to a narrow alley between soundstages where they could talk in private and not draw attention. This wasn't the time for eavesdropping.

"As you know, MGM is always on the lookout to promote from within. If an extra is catching people's attention and that news goes all the way to Mr. Mayer himself, then it's our job at the publicity department to suss things out and make sure they have an upstanding reputation. Do you catch my drift?"

Annabelle started.

"Absolutely." Nathaniel was almost foaming at the mouth, the mere mention of actual fame sending him in a tizzy.

"Now, I have been assisting Clover Halliwell lately and she's mentioned that you two had been friendly in the past, had gone on a few dates. Is that correct?" Annabelle asked, noticing his expression clouding over at the mention of Clover's name.

"Yeah, but she got too clingy, I can't deal with tomatoes like that." He shrugged dismissively.

"Is that so? I believe the letters you've been sending her tell a different story." Annabelle cocked her head. "They show a jealous side that might not go over smoothly with the public."

"What are you driving at?" Nathaniel was getting heated, but she still needed to ask.

"When MGM signs actors to big contracts, there's a morality clause which stipulates that certain behaviours are prohibited. The public wouldn't like knowing a new up-and-comer is sour and harassing a fellow popular actress, especially one who is the talk of the town.Such scandals need to be nipped in the bud. Now tell me, have you been around Clover lately? Say, since she's started filming *The Enchantress*?"

With a suddenness that made her yelp, Nathaniel grabbed her roughly by the arm and pinned her against the wall.

"You think you're slick, don't you? But you're just a silly dame," Nathaniel spat, his face inches from hers. "I've behaved nothing but respectfully toward Clover and what's the thanks I get? She dumps me while she's on her way to the big leagues. What an ungrateful little tease! And for the record, *Speak Easily* started filming the same day as her riveting picture and both have the same schedules so don't you dare try to pin anything on me."

"Let go of me you fool." Annabelle was breathless. Despite having got the answers she was looking for, his grip was tight, and she couldn't wiggle away. She was frightened.

"How about you go complain to your boss and see if he cares." Nathaniel raised his arm to slap her.

That's when that familiar hot tingly wave took over her body, and for once she didn't fight it. Concentrating all her strength on shoving him away, Nathaniel Stanley was thrown off her with surprising force, tumbling over a few feet away in shock.

All Annabelle could do was stare at him with rage in her eyes before letting the anger materialize into words. "Don't you *dare* lay a hand on a woman ever again."

Speechless, Nathaniel scrambled to his feet and disappeared behind the corner, leaving Annabelle alone. Feeling light-headed, she crouched forward, trying to catch her breath. She had felt the power course through her; it was both enthralling and uncontrollable.

She heard a sharp whistling and jerked her head up. It was a young redhead who seemed slightly familiar, but Annabelle couldn't place her at the moment. She was too confused and surprised to think straight.

"Well, that was quite a show." The redhead sauntered over, completely unfazed as she helped Annabelle stand up.

"I-I'm not sure what you're talking about." Annabelle's voice wavered despite her best efforts.

"Oh honey, I saw the whole thing! It was impressive how you flung him away with your mind," the redhead giggled. "It looked like he deserved it."

Chapter 27

Annabelle found herself in a noisy diner near the studio the second after her workday ended. She sat at a booth, anxiously fiddling with the salt and pepper shakers when Mae Hawkes, the mystery dame who saw her telekinetically shove Nathaniel Stanley to the ground, walked toward her. Her nerves only ramped up; she had no idea what would come out of this stranger's mouth. The only thing she knew about her so far was her name.

"Hiya! Have you ordered yet?" Mae spun her head, her red waves swishing around as she tried getting the waiter's attention.

"What can I get you ladies?" He hopped on over, pen and notepad ready.

"I'll have a grilled cheese and a soda," Mae told him then turned her attention to Annabelle. "How about you?"

"I uh ..." Annabelle couldn't recall the last time she was this out of sorts. Could have been at the San Antonio Rodeo Pageant when Maybelle Conway's huge pet pig started running about on stage. Either way, words weren't coming to her.

"She'll have the same, thanks." Mae smiled at the waiter until he walked away.

There was a long moment where both ladies stared at each other. Mae's calm demeanor should have put Annabelle at ease but for some reason it was having the opposite effect. Was this dame going to try blackmailing her or something? She hated not feeling in control of herself like this.

"You must have a lot of questions for me, huh?" Mae asked with a smirk.

"You said it," Annabelle croaked, her voice sounding foreign to her own ears. "How were you not spooked by what you saw? And where did you come from? Which department do you work for?"

"Slow your horses! Let's start at the beginning."

The waiter brought their sodas and Mae took a sip before continuing.

"My name is Mae Hawkes and I'm originally from Ontario, up in Canada. I always loved writing short stories, so I submitted one to an MGM contest and BOOM! I won a train ticket out here and they liked me so much that they hired me as a screenplay assistant about a month ago. I don't get final say on things but I'm learning quite a bit from Frances Marion. It's the eel's hips!"

"How fascinating!" Annabelle's body slowly started relaxing in the booth. Mae looked to be around her age; that winning short story must have been quite something if it brought her all the way out here for a writing position. "But that still doesn't answer my other questions."

"I'm getting to it," Mae chided her as their grilled cheese sandwiches were placed in front of them. "You see, it can be a pain, but scripts often get last-minute changes and it's not unusual for one of us to have to rush over to a soundstage to drop off the latest screenplay ... and that's exactly what I did during the first day of filming for *The Enchantress.*"

And that's when it all clicked in Annabelle's mind. "You were there, you touched the prop book too!"

"Pos-i-tutely!" Mae nodded as she took a bite of her sandwich, the gooey cheese stretching between her mouth and the bread. "I was already running late because I got lost. I'm still new here and the lot is monstrously big, who can blame me? So, when I bent down to pick up the book, the lights went out followed by that bloodcurdling scream and fall. I was spooked and hightailed it out of there! I heard what happened to that poor fella, such a horrible way to go. I tried my best to put that day behind me but then things started happening."

"What kind of things?" Annabelle perked up, sitting on the edge of the booth. "Is it something that made you think you were going crackers?"

"You're right on the money, sister!" Mae looked around, making sure no one was listening to their conversation. "I had a horrible night's sleep after that day. It felt like something was changing within me, deep down, and I woke up utterly drained, as if I had run uphill all night instead of lying in bed. It was preposterously unsettling! And then it started. I would cross fellow employees as I walked about the lot and I swore they said something to me, so I'd turn to acknowledge them and they'd give me a strange look in return, as if they never said anything in the first place. Then one time I walked in front of this extra and he said something rather distasteful about my appearance, so I spun around and gave him hell. But he was adamant he hadn't said anything out loud, mumbling that I was looney and walked around me.

"That's when I started paying closer attention to what I thought I was hearing," Mae continued, happy to have someone's devoted attention. "No one was saying anything to me at all! It's like I was hearing people's thoughts, broadcast to me over a static-filled radio as their mouths remained shut. I was shocked, this had never happened to me before and I don't know anyone else who has this problem other than those phony spiritualists who claim to get messages *from beyond*. But there's no denying that that's exactly what it is. I get bits and pieces here and there, but I can't control it. All I know is that it all started after we touched that book, I would bet my life on it!"

"Well hot damn, I was on the nose with my theory." Annabelle's jaw nearly hit the table. Her frightful encounter with Clover's one-time beau had prevented her from paying closer attention to who this mystery redhead was: the fourth gal who touched that prop. "And that's why you weren't shocked about me sending that fool flying with my mind, because you remembered me touching the book too."

"And there you have it!" Mae raised her palms to the sky, grateful they had finally crossed paths. "I was desperate to find the three of you, but I hadn't the faintest clue how to do that. Have you tracked the others down? Surely, they're experiencing changes too."

"Oh, I found them all right. Milagros is an assistant in the wardrobe department and Velma is Miss Harlow's assistant, lucky gal! But they don't want to discuss that day at all, they've turned on their heels and left me high and dry." Annabelle sighed.

"Hmm, they must not be willing to admit that something

is different with them. Maybe they're scared." Mae frowned. "Well, I guess we'll have to give them some time to come around to the idea."

"Why aren't you scared?" Annabelle asked. "After all, this is unheard of!"

"I find it both scary and thrilling. There must be a reason why this is happening to us. And we'll probably only get to the bottom of it when the other two acknowledge it." Mae shrugged, sipping her soda. "Speaking of scary, why was that extra roughing you up?"

"Golly, well it also stems from that day on the soundstage." Annabelle rolled her eyes, explaining how she was collaborating with Clover to solve Chuck's death. She spilled all the details of what had gone on so far. The only thing she held back was the pregnancy.

"Jiminy Christmas!" Mae smacked her hand on the table, making their plates rattle. "And this all happened during your first week as a publicity assistant? This is an entire screenplay if I do say so myself."

"I guess so," Annabelle chuckled. "Now that Mr. Stanley claims to have an alibi, I need to confirm it before moving forward. It's been a real rollercoaster!"

"You don't say! Well now you have me to help." Mae gave her a knowing smile. "So, what's our next move, partner?"

Annabelle smiled back. It was nice having someone else on her side.

Chapter 28

"It looks like she's the only one in there but it's hard to tell just by looking through the front door," Mae explained as she rounded the corner of the human resources building.

"It's the end of the workday for most of the desk jobs, so I'd bet some kale she's alone in there." Annabelle nodded. "I came in here not too long ago asking to see some papers and I don't think she'd be as kind to search around for me again. She'll start getting wise to my nosy ways. Are you sure you're copacetic about creating a diversion?"

"Sure, I have a knack for it!" Mae waved a hand. "Just try to make it quick, I can't work miracles."

"I'll be quick like a cat." Annabelle gave her a final nod before Mae turned the corner and burst through the building.

"Thank goodness you're here! Most folks have gone home for the day, and I was terribly worried I wouldn't find anyone. I think I saw some sort of mountain lion roam around the lot!" Mae yelped breathlessly.

"A mountain lion on the lot? How the devil could it have gotten in?" the woman behind the front desk asked, not moving from her seat.

"I haven't the faintest idea. Maybe John Barrymore wanted

a companion for his pet chimpanzee, and it got loose?" Mae was upping the frantic energy. "All I know is that it won't look good if human resources knew about it and didn't act while that creature injures someone from the cast and crew. Now let's get a move on!"

The human resources lady grew pale before standing up and following Mae outside, leaving the coast clear for Annabelle to sneak in. She purposefully made loud sounds to see if other employees could be out back, but no one reacted.

"Well, this should be easy-peasy." Annabelle circled the front desk and started searching the back rooms, but she couldn't fully anticipate the volume of papers this department needed to keep on file. She had only seen one small room when she came looking for Chuck Thorne's address, but now she realized it was a maze back here. "Oh brother, I take back what I said."

She didn't have enough time to peruse every room, but before she let the panic settle in she tried to think of how they'd logically sort things. They must have call sheets for every picture that was filmed on the lot, that way they could keep track of who got paid for what.

"I just need to find a cabinet labelled *Speak Easily* and I'll be out of here in a jiffy," Annabelle reassured herself, glancing out the front door where Mae and the human resources employee were out of sight. "Now where are the files for the current pictures located?"

It took her a moment to realize there were labels next to each room specifying the category of filing, and she felt downright silly when she realized one room clearly had *In Production* written next to it. But that feeling was quickly replaced by astonishment when she realized just how many talking pictures were currently being filmed on the MGM lot.

"Gee, this is a well-oiled machine." Annabelle whistled. "Let's see here ... where is this darn picture located? Aha! Here we go, *Speak Easily*."

She opened the cabinet wider, going still for a split second after hearing a noise, then hunching over the files when she realized there wasn't anyone coming back into the building. She flipped through hefty stacks of typewritten notes until she found the daily call sheets with all the cast and crew listed with specific dates and working hours.

"Fiddlesticks," she hissed when she found what she was looking for. Annabelle pulled a slip of paper out of her own pocket and jotted the basics down before closing everything up, making sure the room looked untouched as she made her way back to the front door.

She froze when she noticed the befuddled employee approaching the door with Mae on her heels. Annabelle moved away from the glass, making sure she was out of sight when she heard her new accomplice call out.

"Wait, I think I see it up there in that tree!" Mae yelled as she yanked the employee's arm, making her pivot away from the door. Mae did a stealthy arm wave behind her back, letting Annabelle know she could slip out.

"That is a crow you halfwit," the employee scolded her, losing her patience as Annabelle took the opportunity to slither out the door and around the corner.

"Is that so?" Mae squinted and laughed. "I guess I should wear my cheaters more often! Maybe it wasn't a mountain lion after all! Thanks for being a good sport about it, it's better being safe than sorry. I'll see you around."

The human resources employee mumbled expletives under her breath before stomping back into the building while Mae rounded the corner and met up with Annabelle so they could walk away together.

"I sure hope that was worth the trouble, that dame thinks I'm the biggest dumb Dora on the planet!" Mae guffawed.

"You put on quite the show." Annabelle patted her new friend's shoulder. Not many people would follow through with such antics, but Mae had gumption. It was quite endearing. "Yeah, I found the call sheets and that irate buffoon was telling the truth. He was on the set of *Speak Easily* as an extra the day of Chuck Thorne's death, and by the looks of it he was in some prominent scenes. He couldn't have snuck off without being reprimanded."

"Darn it," Mae groaned. "So where do we stand now? It seems like were back to square one."

"Sure does. He could still be the one sending those scary letters to Clover and Mrs. Thorne but he's not the murderer unless he has an accomplice of sorts." Annabelle sighed as they approached the front gates of the studio. It had been quite the eventful day and she couldn't come up with any grand ideas until she got a good night's rest. "I think I should tell Mr. Beauregard tomorrow. Maybe he would have some insight about how to deal with this blackmailing obsessive."

"Do you think that's wise?" Mae cocked an eyebrow.

"I already know he'll be sore at me for snooping but I'm hoping his need to make sure Clover Halliwell's reputation remains untarnished will overrule his opinion of me," Annabelle explained. "But if you ever hear thought snippets that might be of use, come get me right away."

"Of course." Mae smiled. "Well, I think that's enough excitement for one day. See you tomorrow, partner!"

Annabelle hopped on the Red Car feeling at ease despite the dead end of this investigation. It's crazy how having someone else in your corner can boost your confidence.

Chapter 29

The following morning, Annabelle went about her tasks with an extreme bout of jitters. She was trying to figure out the best time to have a talk with Nelson, but he was always running around in a huff about something or other. If it wasn't about the latest press clippings, then it was about the celebrity antics that would soon be in said press clippings. There was never a convenient time—he was always going to be a little peeved about something! So, Annabelle cornered him right after his lunch; at least he wouldn't be irritably hungry for this chat.

"Mr. Beauregard, could we have a conversation in private?" Annabelle asked as she lightly knocked on his office door.

"What's this about? Did Miss Crawford yell at you too? She's really on a rampage this time." He shook his head in disbelief.

"No, it's nothing like that," Annabelle corrected him as she slowly closed his office door for privacy. "It's about Miss Halliwell and Mr. Thorne's death."

"Now, what did I tell you about that? The coppers ruled it an accident, the fella fell over and that's that. Case closed!" Nelson huffed as he lit another cigarette.

"Yes, well I've uncovered some secrets that make that assessment appear a little doubtful." Annabelle quickly cleared her throat and soldiered on, not giving him a chance to interrupt.

"It turns out the father of Clover's secret unborn child is none other than Chuck Thorne, the deceased—"

"Cheese and crackers!" Nelson yelped, his cigarette falling out of his mouth. Embarrassed, he picked it up before all the scattered papers on his desk could catch fire. "MGM's biggest rising star and a married lighting technician? That is the opposite of an ideal pairing. How did you find out about this?"

"I noticed Clover seemed deeply affected by Chuck's death. Then when I asked her a few questions it became clear they had cared for each other deeply and she confirmed he is the father of her child," Annabelle explained. "Then it got me thinking. What if Louise Thorne, Chuck's widow, knew about this affair? That could be motive enough to want her husband dead. Jealousy can make people do crazy things. But when I talked with her, it pained me to realize she didn't have a clue about her husband's dalliance, let alone an illegitimate child. If anything, although she was grieving, she made it seem like their marriage was almost a platonic one."

"Phew! Well, see? That still means an accident was most likely the reason for Chuck's fall." Mr. Beauregard only relaxed for a moment until he saw Annabelle cock her eyebrow. "There's more, isn't there?"

"And how! Almost simultaneously, I discovered Clover has a deranged fan who sends her obsessive love letters, *and* it turns out Chuck was being blackmailed about his affair. Which means Louise knows about it now, but she doesn't know who the other woman was or about the existence of an imminent love child." Annabelle took a breath; there was so much to tell. "A looney fan on one side and a heartless blackmailer on the other? That sounds too good to be true, so I started to do some digging to confirm they are one and the same. But things got a little complicated when I found a few more of Clover's beaux hidden in her fan mail."

"Oh brother," Mr. Beauregard swooned.

"But not to worry, Clover and I narrowed it down. She was in love with Chuck and says he is undoubtedly the father of her child. The other fellas were just there to pass the time prior to her starting her affair with our dearly departed." Annabelle, paced around the spacious office. "So out of the three casual beaux, we ruled out two based on location and temperament, but the third one seemed like a shoo-in as a deranged fan. His name is Nathaniel Stanley, he's an extra here on the lot, and according to Clover he has a jealous streak. So naturally I asked him a few questions and boy does he have a temper! But it turns out he has a solid alibi—he was filming on a nearby soundstage and couldn't have waltzed over to the set of *The Enchantress* to wreak havoc."

Nelson stared at her, his mouth slightly agape. "And now what?"

"I compared the writing myself. Clover's insane fan and the blackmailer are one and the same," Annabelle said, her mouth getting dry from all the talking. "The few leads we had didn't pan out but whoever is going through all this trouble could surely have pushed Chuck off that railing. And I'm telling you all of this now because I need some publicity department expertise. Have you ever dealt with anything like this before? I have this overwhelming feeling this whole situation will only get worse."

"This is nuts and you're giving me a headache." Nelson

rubbed his temples and pressed on his intercom. "Ginny dear, please get me some aspirin!"

Not even a minute later, Ginny came in with two little white pills in one hand and a glass of water in the other. Mr. Beauregard popped the pills in his mouth, chugged the water, and handed the glass back to his receptionist. Ginny gave Annabelle a smile as she walked back out, doing her best not to seem interested in whatever was going on in this office.

"First off, how are you sure Mrs. Thorne won't blab about this truly unbelievable affair?" Nelson asked the second the door was closed again.

"She won't," Annabelle replied. "Like I said, their marriage was one of convenience and she is rather concerned with appearances. The last thing she'd want to do is air her dirty laundry in public."

"Hmm." Nelson stared at his new employee and shook his head. "I'm perplexed by all of this. You've gone around on this wild goose chase stirring up people's dirty secrets and for what? Sure, a zany blackmailer is bad news, but it still doesn't prove beyond the shadow of a doubt that Chuck was murdered! And you bringing it to my attention is a pain in my behind and will surely lead to some ulcers down the line. If the public doesn't know it, we're in the clear. I don't give a hoot what my employees know, it's what the public knows that's a concern to me. Is that clear?"

"As clear as day." Annabelle bit her tongue. What a waste of time this was. How could he not realize this was a big problem?

"Now how about you get some actual work done instead of sleuthing around? I'm sure there's more paperwork to file away." he dismissed her with a limp wave of his hand.

"What a bunch of baloney," Annabelle mumbled under her breath. "That old grump wouldn't notice a problem if it hit him square in the jaw."

With her tail stuck between her legs, she slithered all the way back to her own office. But she was only halfway into her seat when she heard a strangled yell come from Mr. Beauregard's office.

"What in heaven's name was that?" Ginny asked as she met up with Annabelle in the hallway. Both ladies power walked toward their boss's office where their colleagues were already huddled around.

They all stood there in silence, waiting to figure out what big scandal had befallen this prestigious studio now. Mr. Beauregard yanked open his door, making everyone jump back, then he pointed a shaky finger at Annabelle.

"You better fetch us the evening papers. These headlines are one hell of a catastrophe!" Nelson bellowed.

Chapter 30

An errand boy burst through the door, holding a heavy stack of evening edition newspapers. He barely had time to set them down on a table before Nelson was shoving change in his hand and pushing him out the door.

"Thanks, kid! Now scram, we have a big problem to solve," he said roughly, his hairline damp from stress.

Annabelle picked up the first newspaper on top, and there it was in the headline: CAUGHT IN THE HEADLIGHTS - WIDOW REVEALS LATE HUSBAND HAD AFFAIR WITH CLOVER HALLI-WELL.

"Applesauce!" Annabelle blurted involuntarily. Stunned, she skimmed through the rest of it, her cheeks turning pink with embarrassment. She had just assured her boss there was no way in hell Louise Thorne would squeal about this scandalous affair, yet here it was in bold print for everyone to see.

"All the Los Angeles newspapers mention it, ALL OF THEM!" Nelson shook one newspaper, as if trying to shake the headline right off the page. "The whole city knows about it now. What a mess."

"Well, there's no mention of the pregnancy, at least that's one less scandal to tackle," Annabelle offered. Part of her was afraid Louis B. Mayer himself was going to come barging in here to scold them, and by her boss's frantic state she could tell he felt the same.

"You fool!" He pointed an accusatory finger at her. "You said she had too much pride to talk but here she goes blabbing to anyone who'll listen!"

"Unfortunately, I cannot control how other humans go about their business." His passing of the blame pissed Annabelle off, making her eye twitch. "And might I add you shooed me out of here claiming this wasn't worth your time when I had in fact stated it would only get worse?"

Nelson averted his gaze to the ground like a scolded school-boy. "Something along those lines, yeah."

"And I still stand by what I said. Mrs. Thorne is an extremely private person who enjoys her pristine reputation, it simply doesn't make sense that she would do this." Annabelle tapped her foot on the ground.

"You probably won't hear me say this ever again, but you were right." Nelson sighed, his shoulders sagging in defeat. "But the widow is the least of our problems right now. We need to do some damage control. Fetch all the fellas and Miss Otter, she can take the notes during our emergency meeting."

Annabelle should breathe a sigh of relief that her boss was now on board with all this hullaballoo, but the anxious feeling in the pit of her stomach lingered. She went and told Ginny to meet everyone in the board room, where Mr. Beauregard was pacing all the way at the front of the lengthy thick oak table. He had placed the stack of evening editions on the table and gestured for them to have a look.

"Well, this isn't good," Cooper whistled, *Los Angeles Times* in hand.

"These reporters sure had a field day with the headlines, they all have something to do with lighting," another older, grouchier colleague chimed in.

"It's in such poor taste! After all, the man was pushed to his death," Annabelle blurted, suddenly wondering if her temperamental telekinetic abilities had suddenly transferred to her tongue.

"Pushed?" Her colleagues nearly said in unison, judgement and surprise written all over their faces. Ginny was the only one not startled by this statement.

"Yeah, yeah, Miss Stonewood has some theories we can tackle later." Nelson waved his hand like an eccentric magician trying to make something disappear. "Right now, we need to make sure Miss Halliwell's reputation doesn't take too much of a hit. MGM has put a lot of time, effort, and not to mention money into boosting her career. Her latest picture could bomb horribly if we don't salvage this situation! Let's put our thinking caps on and come up with a solution."

Then a deluge of ridiculous suggestions ensued:

"We could make a statement saying the widow is looney, looking for her five minutes of fame. I'm sure we could make it real convincing."

"We could say she's a lying drunk, as simple as that."

"We could pretend like this was all part of some elaborate studio contest and the poor lady was too daft to understand it."

Annabelle listened to these clueless men shooting off ideas, which only got dumber and dumber, until her blood was boiling over.

"Why are your instincts to throw Mrs. Thorne under the bus? And why bother denying a very factual affair?"

They all just stared at her as if she had two heads and was speaking a foreign language only Ginny seemed to understand.

"How are you going to keep track of anything if you keep piling lies on top of it? Surely the reporters will poke some holes in it sooner or later! Wouldn't the best thing be to release a statement saying the affair happened and spin it from there while keeping the press away from Miss Halliwell?"

Her colleagues turned to their boss, waiting to see his reaction, but he seemed just as flustered as they were.

"Uh, I agree with keeping those vultures away from Miss Halliwell, she's much too delicate to deal with them right now. She needs to focus on her latest picture." Nelson nodded, lighting a new cigarette. "But we don't need to admit anything, not yet. We don't need to bite off more than we can chew. It's best to be aloof in these situations—trust me I've been doing this much longer than you."

Annabelle bit her tongue. She wasn't going to win this battle. Before she could tamper her emotions or think of what she was doing, the cigarette she was staring at in Nelson's hand burnt all the way down to his fingers in a split second, making him yelp.

"Holy Moses, that's never happened before!" Nelson shoved his fingers in a nearby cup of water for relief.

"I'll go get an ointment," Annabelle said before scurrying out of the conference room, Ginny giving her a concerned look as she walked by her.

Mindlessly, Annabelle stomped all the way outside and kept on going. She'd find the nurse's room eventually, but she intended to take her time.

"That bunch of hyenas are only looking at this mess from one angle and it's the least important one!" Annabelle huffed, her southern twang more pronounced when she was worked up. They were only looking at the cover of the book when the content was actually much more important. "So much for getting any actual help with solving poor Chuck's murder. I can't believe I even thought for a second Mr. Beauregard would loop in the coppers. Shame on me for expecting decency!"

The only thing that calmed her down somewhat was knowing she could talk to Mae about this. And hopefully they could put her mind-reading abilities to good use before things truly went off the rails.

Chapter 31

"Golly, that's one hell of a day," Mae whistled as Annabelle filled her in on the latest developments. Now they were walking over to Clover's dressing room to check up on her, having found excuses to wander out of their respective departments. "She must be a wreck about this."

"Wouldn't you be? There's more to it than Louise simply blabbing to the press, there's got to be," Annabelle mused. "Isn't it a laugh that there's an MGM-level drama picture happening behind the scenes at the studio and the head of publicity doesn't give a hoot about it?"

"Yeah, sounds to me like he's only thinking about how it affects him and his job." Mae rolled her eyes.

"We're an unlikely couple of investigators but at least we're trying to get to the bottom of it," Annabelle reassured her friend as they walked up the stairs to the second-storey dressing rooms.

She knocked on the door and a croaking voice told her to come in. Annabelle peeked inside only to see Clover being comforted by none other than Jean Harlow. Both ladies were seated on the couch with the blonde bombshell placing a reassuring hand on the shoulder of the rising star.

159

"Oh, I'm sorry to interrupt," Annabelle blurted, glancing at them. "We'll wait outside."

She shut the door softly and turned to Mae. "Miss Harlow is in there with her! I guess they're closer than I thought."

"You don't say!" Mae cocked an eyebrow and lowered her voice. "You know, every time we work on a script for one of her movies, the fellas always want to rely on her sensuality. But the truth is she has perfect comedic timing! Believe me, what I've gleaned from their thoughts proves those men have a one-track mind."

"Her assistant Velma is one of the other gals that touched that prop book with us and boy does she seem like the opposite of Jean Harlow in every way imaginable. My alarm clock is less rude than her," Annabelle quipped, then stood upright when she saw a familiar face approach the dressing room building. "And speaking of comedic timing, here she comes!"

"Is that so?" Mae tried to glance discreetly. "She kinda looks like Louise Brooks or Colleen Moore with that black bobbed haircut, doesn't she?"

"Shush, she's coming up." Annabelle swatted her friend's arm.

Velma walked up the stairs to the second floor, gracing them with a ghost of a smile before knocking on Clover's door. She poked her head inside. "I'm terribly sorry to interrupt but Jean, you have that photography session with George Hurrell in half an hour. We need to get ready."

She shut the door and now the three assistants stood around awkwardly, looking anywhere other than at each other, the prop book looming over them like a thunderous cloud about to erupt.

"It's nice of Miss Harlow to console Miss Halliwell," Annabelle said after clearing her throat. "This is Mae Hawkes, an assistant with the screenplay department. She was also there during the first day of filming *The Enchantress*."

"How do you do?" Velma replied coolly.

"How lovely to meet you! I think we have more in common than you realize. Annabelle and I certainly made that discovery." Mae was unfazed by Velma's distant attitude and tried prodding. She tried to pick up some of her thoughts but alas it didn't switch on and off like a radio.

"I don't think so," Velma replied sharply.

The door to Clover's dressing room flung open and Jean Harlow came out, radiant without a stitch of makeup on.

"Thank you for coming to fetch me, Velma, it had slipped my mind." Jean turned her attention to Annabelle. "You must be Miss Stonewood. Clover has told me all about you. It's very gracious of you to check up on her when you're already busy working under Mr. Beauregard. He's quite the grouch, isn't he?"

"He can be," Annabelle replied, Mae elbowing her to be formerly introduced. "This is my friend Mae, she works in the screenplay department."

"Nice to meet you! I'm pleased that they're hiring more dames to help with the scripts. Some of the dialogue men write for me is absolute nonsense." Jean shook her head.

"We're currently working on your next picture, *Red-Headed Woman*. It'll be a hit!" Mae answered giddily.

"Glad to hear it! Anyhoo, I should get ready for my photography session. It was swell meeting you." Jean flashed them a smile before leaving with Velma, who didn't bother saying goodbye to them.

"Isn't she the cat's pyjamas?" Mae sighed, starstruck. "It's too bad her assistant has a lousy attitude, but she'll come around."

"Yeah, I'm not so sure about that." Annabelle shrugged. "Let's put that aside for now, we have more pressing matters to tend to."

Annabelle slipped inside the dressing room followed by Mae, seeing Clover still hunched over on the couch, dabbing her eyes with a handkerchief. Despite her despair, she noted the star was still expertly concealing her growing belly.

"Hi Clover, I came over as soon as I could get away from Mr. Beauregard." Annabelle followed Clover's gaze which was quizzically fixed on Mae.

"I'm Mae Hawkes from the screenplay department. It's a pleasure meeting you, despite the circumstances. Annabelle has filled me in on your harrowing situation and I'll try my damnedest to help you," Mae offered. "It must be a nightmare having your personal life broadcast to the world like this."

"I'm surprised Louise did this, it's very out of character," Annabelle chimed in, relieved Clover wasn't balking at Mae's presence.

"You'll be less surprised after I show you this." Clover grabbed a typewritten letter from her coffee table and handed it over. "It looks like my abominable admirer wasn't too happy I didn't reach out to him after he murdered Chuck."

Both Annabelle and Mae hunched over the scathing letter where this man boldly admits to murder then expected Clover to come crawling over to him. Incensed by Clover's radio silence, he went to Chuck's widow and spilled the beans.

162

"Well, this is beyond delusional," Mae commented. "He's playing everyone like a bunch of marionettes, playing God by pulling the strings!"

"What makes me real sore is that he admits *in writing* that he's killed Chuck, yet I know Mr. Beauregard and the coppers won't bat an eye at it," Annabelle said morosely. "To them this will just be a letter written by some deranged fan, it won't hold any weight. People can write anything after all."

"At least we know better," Mae replied, shaking her head in disbelief. "Maybe we should be in charge around here instead of these dum-dums who can't connect the pieces of the puzzle."

"Didn't you say Louise wasn't overly fussed about the affair? Would she really be that outraged that I was the other woman?" Clover asked indignantly. "My entire reputation is crumbling to pieces around me because of this."

"See, that's the part that doesn't make sense to me." Annabelle put the letter back on the table and paced the room. "She didn't want to make a fuss about it, so why did she go against her word? I think we need to go talk with her, all of us. That way we can get the full picture and restore your image in the public's eye."

"Oh, I'm not so sure that's a great idea." Clover shook her head nervously. "Those vultures will be tailing me, waiting to take pictures or worse!"

"We'll get you a good disguise and you'll blend in with us lowly MGM crew members," Annabelle reassured her. "And we should do it tonight. My lovely colleagues are planning a smear campaign against Louise and it's not sitting well with me."

"Fair enough," Clover sighed. "The quicker we handle this, the faster I stop being a puppet in this swine's games."

"That's the spirit!" Mae chimed in exuberantly. "Now let's

163

get you a swell disguise, shall we?"

Chapter 32

"They should be here any minute," Annabelle said as she glanced at her watch. She stood in front of her boarding house with Mae, and they were both waiting for Clover and Louise to arrive for what could only be an uncomfortable conversation. "Are you sure your diversion was successful?"

"For the last time, yes! Those reporters thought I was the real deal and they followed me all the way to Venice Beach and then I hightailed it out of there. That was hours ago, and they still think 'Miss Halliwell' is out there somewhere," Mae explained. "I can't believe the red hair fooled them."

"You're right, I just have the jitters." Annabelle shook her hands as if trying to fling off bugs. "I certainly hope they find the place easily."

After tossing out innumerable suggestions for a meet-up location, they settled on Annabelle's boarding house because it wasn't a public place, and it wouldn't be on those newspaper hounds' radar. Plus, her elusive, night owl neighbours wouldn't be nosy.

As the sun began its descent, the first cab pulled up to the curb and a dowdier version of Clover Halliwell stepped out. She had a matronly brown wig pinned back in an updo popular at the turn of the century, a thick set of cheaters, and a black shapeless dress that more than concealed her biggest secret.

"I hope I'm not late," she said as she approached, seeming uncomfortable to don a costume when not on set. "Has she arrived yet? Jeepers, I'm a basket case!"

"Take a deep breath and remember we need to do this for Chuck's benefit." Annabelle grabbed Clover's hands to reassure her, putting her own nerves to the side.

"That must be her now," Mae announced, making them all spin around to face the road.

Louise Thorne also jumped out of a cab wearing dark sunglasses and a cloche hat pulled down low to conceal her face. It wasn't as elaborate as Clover's disguise, but it did the trick. She joined the three of them on the sidewalk, everyone at a loss for words for a solid minute.

"Let's go upstairs to my room, shall we?" Annabelle cleared her throat and led the way.

As they walked up the rickety stairs to the second floor, Annabelle couldn't help but stifle a giggle. Having a kooky colleague, a widow, and her late husband's famous mistress as her first ever guests in this big city was unconventional to say the least.

"It isn't much, but it'll have to do under these circumstances," she said sheepishly, realizing it was smaller than Clover's dressing room and not as well furnished.

"Nonsense, it's very kind of you to host us for this conversation. We need to clear the air," Louise said, her inscrutable gaze setting on Clover. "I guess we both have some explaining to do."

Annabelle and Mae exchanged a worried look, wondering if they'd have to break off a brawl. What if this had been a terrible idea? They held their breath as the two women in Chuck Thorne's life held eye contact, their disguises still firmly in place.

"I want to extend my condolences and apologize in the same breath." Clover cleared her throat, adjusting the comically round glasses framing her eyes. "As Chuck's wife, this must all be very difficult for you. Our relationship started in earnest, with no malicious intent toward you. In fact, he spoke highly of you and explained that your marriage wasn't grounded in love, and I must admit that eased some of my guilt, even if deep down I knew there was a possibility he was pulling my leg. It might be silly, but I trusted him wholeheartedly and we cared deeply for each other. I respect you as a woman and I'm saddened to see our secrets out in the open for the world to judge."

For an agonizingly long moment, Louise stared straight ahead with a stony expression that made Annabelle's heart fall into her stomach. This was it, the moment the widow snapped, perfect fodder for the gossip columns. But instead, Louise sighed and took off her hat, raking her hands through her hair and gave her husband's mistress an apologetic smile.

"Isn't this a grand old mess?" Louise started. "Rest assured Chuck wasn't lying when he said we weren't in love. Don't get me wrong, we were very fond of each other, but it was more like a friendship than anything else. Our marriage allowed me to be comfortable and I enjoyed it, but it did cross my mind that Chuck could be seeing someone on the side. Once Annabelle and I found those letters from the blackmailer after Chuck's death, the affair didn't bother me as long as it remained in the shadows. Boy was I silly to think it wouldn't come back to bite me in the rear."

"Wait, then why did you tell all of Los Angeles about it?" Clover frowned, her cheeks flushing.

"This is the tough part—and I hate being vulnerable." Louise took a deep breath. "Chuck was the main breadwinner. I taught at schools here and there, but it was pennies compared to his studio salary. And now that he's gone ... let's just say I'm struggling for cash. I've been scrambling, trying to find a solution that doesn't involve selling our house, when out of nowhere that blackmailer sends me a letter. He said he would give me a hefty amount of dough if I told everyone Chuck was having an affair with Clover Halliwell prior to his death." Her voice wavered. "I had no idea if it was true, but I was frightened and desperate! I was afraid of what would happen if I said no to him. I'm the one that owes you a big apology. I've made everything worse."

Without a moment's hesitation, Clover walked over to Louise and embraced her, cutting all the tension from the room. Annabelle bet this was a moment the blackmailer wasn't anticipating.

"I had a feeling there was a reason behind your decision to go public." Annabelle nodded. "That lowlife! He's using you to destroy Clover's reputation because he's obsessed with her."

"So now that that's all cleared up, what's the next step?" Mae asked. "This ghoul is on a rampage, and something tells me he won't stop until Clover becomes his."

"How awful," Clover and Louise said in unison.

"We need to look at the bigger picture," Annabelle said, looking out her window to see the sun had fully set and the stars were coming out. "He could have kept a low profile after pushing Chuck, but he's persisted in making things worse. His mind is set on a revenge, and we need to use it to our advantage. By pretending to play by his rules, we can trip him up and corner him. It might be scary, but we have to be bold. We're the only ones who want to properly solve this mess. Are y'all with me?"

The four dames exchanged conspiratorial grins.

"Pos-i-tutely!" Clover spoke for the group.

Chapter 33

"It's official, this place has turned into a zoo! Good luck," Ginny exclaimed as she patted Annabelle on the shoulder and scurried off to tend to a mess of file folders left by a reckless employee.

Annabelle was only a few footsteps into the publicity department; the whole building hummed with nervous energy and muffled phone calls. She peeked into every office as she headed for her own, and all her colleagues were fielding what she could only imagine were aggressive calls from reporters. This whole Clover Halliwell/Chuck Thorne scandal wasn't going to blow over quickly, and they didn't even know about the murder angle!

She stood in the doorway of Mr. Beauregard's office. He was also on the phone and only briefly nodded at her before shifting around, turning his back to the employee who raised the alarm about this whole mess.

"No matter, I have an important assignment of my own to contend with," Annabelle mumbled as she turned on her heels.

She could ascertain that her boss respected her a little—enough to keep her around. Yet he didn't respect her enough to give her any credit or tap into her full set of skills. His male ego certainly got in the way of properly handling the situation but that was his problem. Despite yesterday being an utter circus and having to orchestrate a difficult conversation with two women who appeared at odds, Annabelle felt confident.

The one-sided conversations she heard on her way back to her office made her both giggle and cringe:

"It's a load of baloney! That poor widow is known to be a pathological liar, Mr. Thorne mentioned it all the time ... Uh, yes, I realize that can't be confirmed since he's dead ... "

"That poor lady is just jealous and wants to be a big star herself. Doesn't everyone want to be famous?"

"Of course, we're denying it! You're a bunch of fools for thinking there's any truth behind this. Aren't you lot supposed to be professionals?"

Annabelle closed her office door, muffling the desperate lies her colleagues were peddling. "They certainly are grasping at straws."

She took out a notepad and fountain pen and placed them in front of her, closing her eyes to review all the information at hand. The thought slipped into her mind that despite last night's high stress conversation, she hadn't had a telekinetic episode in front of Louise and Clover in her apartment. She calmly set the thought aside before reacting to it—she could only handle one crisis at a time!

"Focus, Annabelle, you need to concoct a convincing letter," she scolded herself, rolling her neck to work out the creeping tension that had set there. It has to strike the right balance, not too cajoling or demanding. He needs to buy it.

After about an hour of brainstorming, she looked down at her notes and felt satisfied this would do the trick.

"I'm not sure it matters because they're all pretty tied up with the phone lines, but I'm going over to see Miss Halliwell if anyone is looking for me," Annabelle told Ginny as she walked by the front desk.

"Very well. Oh, and Annabelle?" Ginny's words made her stop in her tracks. "I don't know the full extent of what's going on, but I wanted to say I find it admirable of you to look out for Miss Halliwell. These fellas here are trying to save their behinds, but I can tell you have better intentions. I hope this chaos gets sorted out soon."

"Gee, thanks Ginny! That's very kind of you." Annabelle gave her a smile. "We should have a proper lunch together once the dust settles. We can get a chance to chat more than a few sentences here and there."

"Pos-i-tutely!" Ginny nodded.

On that jolly note, Annabelle headed across the lot to the lion's den. Once those newspapers hit the pavement late yesterday with those big scalding headlines, Clover and her dressing room were heavily guarded, and rightfully so. Her reputation could take a bigger nosedive if the public knew the full extent of her relationship with Chuck, and *that* secret still seemed to be contained to Mr. Beauregard and herself.

"I'm Miss Stonewood from the publicity department. Miss Halliwell is expecting me," Annabelle fibbed as she flashed her flimsy credentials. Luckily the security guard recognized her and let her in.

"It's so nice to see a familiar face, all these guards are giving me the creeps!" Clover shivered as she stood up from her makeup chair where she was brushing her copper tresses. Her eyes settled on Annabelle's notebook. "I think I know what you're here to deliver."

"As promised!" Annabelle chirped, making a mental note to tone down her giddiness. They were trying to frame a murderer after all, this wasn't Christmas morning.

"Hand it over then," Clover sighed and extended her hand, Annabelle placing the notebook in her grasp. The rising star took a few minutes to read through it, her other hand instinctively caressing her belly. "Do you think this'll work? What if he smells a rat and retaliates in a bigger fashion? We have a lot riding on this."

"And how!" Annabelle huffed, hands on hips. "We can't just wait around like sitting ducks for him to launch another attack! It's time to be bold and this is the way to do it. It's *you* he wants, so by making him believe you're finally his, it gives us a chance to ambush him."

"And you want me to write this out word for word on my stationery?" Clover replied after a moment of contemplation, the plan truly sinking in.

"Yes, it needs to come from you, on your paper with your handwriting. It's an important detail," Annabelle explained. "This is the only thing I ask of you, the rest will be taken care of by Mae and myself. You can trust us."

Clover went back to her makeup table and pulled out her fancy stationery set. She took her time writing the letter, giving her signature a fancy flourish before sealing it in an envelope and spritzing it with perfume as an extra special touch. Her gaze was intensely fiery as she handed the letter over to Annabelle. "Let's get this bastard."

Chapter 34

"They sure are grouchy in there! Do you think they always wake up on the wrong side of the bed?" Mae groaned.

"Well as long as the letter gets sent, that's all that matters to me right now," Annabelle replied. They went together to the fan mail department to deliver Clover's letter to her delusional admirer and now both of them had an anxious energy they couldn't shake.

"It would have saved us quite a bit of time if he had simply written his address on his letters instead of a postal box." Mae shook her head. "This whole hullabaloo would have been over and done with in record time."

"No such luck, pal. Say, do you want to go to the commissary? I think we deserve some ice cream sandwiches," Annabelle offered. "My treat."

"I won't say no to that!" Mae exclaimed. "Good thing we're not in front of the cameras, they'd be monitoring every bite we take."

"Goodness, and I thought pageants could be tough! I love ice cream too much to subject myself to a strict diet," Annabelle giggled as the two of them made their way to the commissary, practically drooling.

Their words rang especially true when a sea of extras and actresses eyed them begrudgingly as they waltzed by the cafeteria seating area with their ice cream sandwiches in hand. They hung out in the shade outside the building, enjoying their treats, when they noticed a familiar face walk on by.

"Oh, that's Milagros from the wardrobe department!" Annabelle pointed like a child. "Maybe we should—"

"Milagros!" Mae yelled unapologetically. "Come over here, will ya?"

Startled, the raven-haired assistant approached them with hesitation. Annabelle noticed the same reluctance and fear in her eyes; she didn't know how to start this conversation.

"Nice day, isn't it?" Annabelle blurted, wanting to kick herself for such bland small talk when there was so much to discuss. "This is Mae Hawkes, she's an assistant in the screenplay department."

"It's a pleasure meeting you officially," Mae extended her hand. "Although we did meet when we touched that prop book on the set of *The Enchantress*."

Milagros had started reaching out to shake Mae's hand but retracted it once the book was mentioned. There was no doubt this topic was still off limits with her, but Mae pressed on.

"Look, we know this is pos-i-tutely zany, but have you developed any *abilities* since then?" Mae looked around and lowered her voice. "Annabelle here can move things with her mind, and I can read thoughts. Isn't that neat?"

"I-I should get back to work. There's a whole slew of revolution-era dresses that need to be sewed." Milagros took a few steps back, as if backing away from a rabid dog.

"Wouldn't it be strange that we both gained these abilities, and you got squat?" Mae continued, making Annabelle groan. "Surely there's something you're keeping from us!"

"I don't know what kind of game this is, but I want no part of it!" Milagros spat as she turned on her heels to leave.

"See what you've done? Now she'll never talk to us again," Annabelle scolded her new friend. She had come to understand that Mae was a no-nonsense gal who didn't always think things all the way through, and this was definitely one of those times.

"Oh, don't cast a kitten. She'll—" Mae stopped mid-sentence and went into a strange trance, her whole body going rigid as her eyes fluttered wildly. She was even muttering nonsense like she was possessed! It gave Annabelle a proper fright.

"Mae! Mae, what's wrong?" Annabelle whisper-yelled, trying not to draw attention from the continuous traffic going in and out of the commissary. She wasn't sure if she should reach out and touch her or let her be. "Are you ill? Should I fetch a doctor?"

"... ball of fire." Mae snapped out of her trance and immediately started power walking after Milagros, leaving a dumbfounded Annabelle behind. "Why are you so concerned about balls of fire?"

Milagros looked horribly faint as she turned around to face her. "What on earth are you talking about?"

"Jeepers, Mae, what has gotten into you?" Annabelle exclaimed as she caught up with them.

"Milagros here has been thinking about balls of fire. She's afraid one will show up in her hand again. Isn't that right?" Mae looked at her expectantly, as if what she said wasn't absolutely bonkers.

"I didn't say anything of the sort," Milagros croaked, hiding her hands behind her back.

"You didn't have to honey, I heard your thoughts." Mae tapped her head, in case they didn't know where thoughts came from. "You also thought about turning Isadora's glass of water into ice and shattering everywhere. Who's Isadora?"

"Isadora is my younger sister! *Dios mío!*" Milagros clapped her hands over her mouth to muffle an onslaught of profanities. "I can't believe this is happening."

"Wait a minute, so that whole spooky display was you reading thoughts?" Annabelle asked incredulously. "You gave me the heebie-jeebies!"

"Oh applesauce! Don't make such a fuss about it." Mae waved a dismissive hand.

"Mae, sweetheart, your whole body went as stiff as a board and your eyes nearly rolled back in your head. It looked like you were trying to imitate Frankenstein's monster!" Annabelle exclaimed. "You'll be the laughingstock of this studio if you keep that up."

"*Anyhoo*, we can discuss that later." Mae turned her attention back to a shell-shocked Milagros, putting her hands gently on her shoulders. "I know this is a lot to take in. I suggest we go somewhere quiet so we can talk it over. Would you be all right with that?"

Milagros' eyes kept darting from Mae to Annabelle for what felt like forever; it almost looked like she was trying with all her might to not pass out. Then her shoulders slowly relaxed and some colour came back into her cheeks.

"I know a secluded spot where we won't be bothered,"

Milagros finally said. Annabelle and Mae sighed with relief.

Chapter 35

"Gee, it almost looks like we're in the Big Apple if you don't look over here," Mae pointed out.

The three of them—Annabelle, Milagros, and Mae—were hovering by the manmade lake on the outdoor New York City set of Central Park on the MGM lot, the soundstages, and other sets still visible to the left, in the distance. This spot was secluded enough for them to have this strange conversation. The two friends remained patient, keeping things light as Milagros worked up the nerve to tell them about what had happened.

"That night after we touched that book, I had the strangest dreams," Milagros finally started, eyes fixed on the lake. "I felt something fighting within me, this powerful energy, and I woke up exhausted. I've had puzzling dreams before, but this was beyond all of that. I didn't notice anything different at first but then these unexplainable things would happen when I tended to the wardrobe ..."

"For goodness' sake, tell us!" Mae blurted after another few minutes of silence. "The anticipation is killing me."

"Hush up, will you?" Annabelle scolded her.

"That's all right, I need to work on being more assertive." Milagros stood up straighter and took a deep breath. "It started with the clothes irons and steamers going wonky. I'd pour the water in, and it would either splash out everywhere, refusing to turn into steam, or it would turn into ice and break the gadgets. I thought it was a widespread problem within our building, but then I got scolded and realized it only happened to the ones I touched." She fiddled nervously with her long black hair. "Then it was the phone lines that started acting up. We're all told that whoever is closest to it should answer, but when I did sparks would go off and the line would go dead. They had to bring in the electrician to see what was what, and he couldn't find anything wrong! So, I've been told to stay away from the phone. And then there's the fire ball incident, that's the scariest of them all."

"Golly, what happened?" Annabelle encouraged Milagros, seeing her falter a little.

"Well, one day earlier this week, all my colleagues were huddled up together and they were talking about me, laughing at me because I'm the odd one out. I was listening to them from a safe distance and thankfully they didn't notice me because all of a sudden, my right hand got blistering hot and when I looked down, I saw this tiny ball of flames hovering in my hand," Milagros explained. "I didn't know what to do, this wasn't a normal occurrence! So, I smacked my hand against the wall as if killing a bug and I hightailed it out of there to cool down. Up until that point, I didn't want to admit to myself that this was a problem, but I couldn't ignore that ball of flames."

"Well, I'll be damned," Mae's eyes went wide as she turned to her friend. "It sure sounds similar to your telekinetic abilities."

"I'm not so sure about that, I haven't made things appear in my hands," Annabelle mused. "What would you call it

Milagros?"

"There's a *brujeria* tradition in Mexico where my family is from. My mother is afraid of all that spooky talk, which only made me all the more curious about it growing up," Milagros explained. "According to some books and word of mouth, I think I narrowed down what is going on. I can't believe I'm saying this, but I can conjure up the elements. I've already done it with water and ice, electricity, and now fire. It all adds up!"

"Jeepers, I had never even heard of that before now." Mae was practically giddy with this big development. "And what were the odds that a quiet mouse like you gets an active ability like that? I guess the universe decided I was too much of a loudmouth and stuck me with reading other people's thoughts."

"Sure, it's all fun and games until you accidentally injure someone innocent!" Annabelle scoffed, turning to Milagros. "I don't know about you but that sends me into a panic."

"Me too," Milagros nodded. "So now what? Clearly, we can't control these newfound abilities."

"We're in a bit of a jam until Velma, Jean Harlow's assistant, reaches out to us," Annabelle sighed. "She's the other gal who touched that book and she's the last piece of the puzzle. But let's just say she's a little prickly."

"I'll say! She's as cold as Antarctica!" Mae smirked. "I bet old Saint Nick himself would be afraid of her icy demeanor."

"So, let's put that on ice for now." Annabelle stifled a giggle, pleased with her pun. "We do have a more pressing issue to tend to. Remember how I mentioned Chuck Thorne was possibly pushed off the balcony on that soundstage? Well, it turns out I was right and now this monster is blackmailing Chuck's widow and threatening Clover Halliwell."

"Oh!" Milagros's hand flew to her chest in surprise. "Deary me, what a circus."

"You're right on the money with that one, it's an absolute merry-go-round," Mae added. "But we've set a plan in motion, an ambush of sorts."

"We decided enough was enough, this bozo has done more than his share of damage and now we're simply going to return the favour and catch him red-handed," Annabelle added. "But we would need your help. As Mae so eloquently put it, she has a more passive power. But if you join us, at least we'll be two out of three with the ability to defend ourselves with our minds, even if they're unruly."

"Sheesh, no need to rub it in." Mae crossed her arms and pouted.

"I know it's a lot to ask, but no one else is acknowledging this situation or willing to stick their necks out. Plus, we'd get a better understanding of our abilities if we're together, not to mention put a stop to this murdering blackmailer," Annabelle pleaded. "What do ya say?"

Milagros stared into the lake again, watching her reflection sway. She felt like she had been slapped in the face with a whole new scary reality, yet she knew what she had to say. "All right, I agree to help you out. But I want a detailed explanation of what your plan is, I don't want us to show up unprepared."

"That's swell! And don't you worry, I have it all planned out," Annabelle said with a wink.

"You're the berries!" Mae hopped over to Milagros and embraced her in a one-sided hug. "You're now a member of our little investigation team!"

Chapter 36

"This sure is a snazzy car," Mae mused as she touched every-thing within sight from her spot in the passenger seat. "It's real nice of Clover to have lent it to us."

"Well, we needed it to make this whole thing appear genuine, so she didn't have much of a choice," Annabelle guffawed from the driver's seat, her silk-gloved hands gripping the steering wheel tight. "Are we nearly there, Milagros?"

"Yes, there's one last left turn coming up and we'll be at the X on the map," Milagros replied as she followed the outlined path on the Los Angeles map in her lap.

The three of them were in Clover Halliwell's pristine, black 1932 Cadillac Lasalle and they were making the trek through Beachwood Canyon and partially up Mount Lee where their designated meeting spot was located. Annabelle made that last turn smoothly, not wanting to damage this borrowed celebrity car, and cut the engine. They were parked in a small clearing, the edge of a cliff close by with beautiful scenic views of the city stretching out ahead and presumably below.

"Right, so even if he notices the car, it's not a big deal since it's Clover's. It wouldn't send off alarm bells in his mind,"

Annabelle explained, adjusting her gloves to glance at her watch. "We have enough time to get up there and get in position before he shows up. It's important that he doesn't notice you gals. He's under the impression Clover is meeting him alone."

The three of them got out of the car and Annabelle fiddled with her red wig. Since they weren't going to send poor Clover into the lion's den, Annabelle would act as the rising star for this daring plan. She borrowed a wig, a smart outfit, and a pair of white-framed sunglasses which were becoming all the rage with the big MGM names.

"I gotta hand it to ya, you do look like Miss Halliwell." Mae looked her up and down. "As long as he doesn't get too close."

"Unfortunately, I have an inkling he will try to get uncomfortably chummy with me. But that's why we have these." Annabelle pulled a prop pocket pistol out of her coat pocket and so did her accomplices. "Once I pull mine out, y'all can come out of your hiding spots with your props raised. Do you have the rope?"

"Yes," both Mae and Milagros replied, showing the item hidden in the lining of their coats.

"All right, let's ankle." Annabelle led the way as they walked up part of Mount Lee.

They walked in silence for about ten minutes, the only sounds were their breathing and the crunching of the ground under their feet. The grim reality of what they were attempting to do here was settling in, but they were all committed to ending this nightmare once and for all. This fella can't just manipulate women willy-nilly when he doesn't get what he wants. He needed to be stopped and this was as good a way as any. Sure, it was unconventional, but nothing about this scenario was by the numbers.

The small trail opened up and there it stood looming over them, the *Hollywoodland* sign. Despite the late afternoon sun, the big white block letters glared against the woodsy foliage surrounding it. The three women took a moment to stare up at it, gobsmacked by its size and stature in Hollywood folklore. It was impressive to say the least.

"That's enough staring." Annabelle cleared her throat, snapping them back to reality. "Mae, go hide behind the H and Milagros you can go behind the W. And make sure you're hidden from all angles!"

"You got it, boss," Mae teased as she patted her friend's shoulder. "Good luck."

Milagros gave Annabelle's hands a reassuring squeeze before heading toward the W. The three of them, unlikely, inexperienced accomplices, were all set and ready to ambush a self-appointed murderer and blackmailer.

"It's show time," Annabelle exhaled. This was no small feat, yet it was clear they were the ones for the job. Now they'd have to see how it all unfolded.

As she paced in front of the prestigious landmark, Annabelle tried to remain in character, emulating a version of Clover Halliwell who would finally succumb to the appeal of a man who murdered the father of her unborn child and got a kick out of blackmailing a widow. It was a gigantic stretch of the imagination and forced her to tap into her days as an extra, even though she was never given such a high-risk assignment in front of the cameras or otherwise.

"He should be here by now," Annabelle hissed through

clenched teeth as the minutes stretched on and the sun started setting in the distance. For all she knew, he was a man who enjoyed being fashionably late. But this would interfere with the rest of her plan.

As time ticked by, it became obvious that neither the perpetrator nor Mr. Beauregard and the coppers she had requested by letter to show up, were remotely punctual. Annabelle bit her tongue, holding in the cussing she wanted to let loose. Why on earth did she think she could concoct a plan and control a situation which could only be described as unpredictable at best and a ticking time bomb at its worse?

"This is what happens when you try calling the shots for a loose cannon." Annabelle sighed grimly after noticing they had been waiting around for two hours. She raised her voice to get her friends' attention. "All right, ladies. Let's call it a day. This guy is a no-show."

Mae and Milagros popped out from behind their gigantic, assigned letters and approached the fake Clover Halliwell who looked more than defeated.

"It was a good effort," Mae offered. "But this fella is unhinged! We can try wracking our brains all we want but it'll be impossible to predict his behaviour."

"Maybe it's for the best," Milagros chimed in. "This could be the universe trying to save our necks."

"I suppose so. Anyhoo, let's get back to the car. I bet Clover's nerves are through the roof waiting to hear about this," Annabelle said as she headed for the path down the hill.

Both disappointed and relieved, the three friends made it back to the high-end car. They were about to open their respective doors, eager to head back to safer ground, when they heard a rustling in the trees to their right. They noticed the barrel of a gun before the full figure emerged in front of them.

"Surprise! And you dames thought I wouldn't show up to this clam bake," the figure announced, leaving them stunned.

Chapter 37

"Who the devil is that?" Mae whisper-yelled a few feet from Annabelle, not daring to move.

"You know, for a moment I truly believed my darling Clover would be here. If I became so lovestruck for her, the same could happen the other way around, couldn't it?" the killer asked, gun still trained on them. "Naturally I spied on you from a distance. Sure, you look like her on the surface, but you certainly don't move around like her. Not quite as elegant."

"Hey, I take offense at that!" Annabelle spat, her southern pageant upbringing wounded. "And I can't believe you, Cooper Mason, are responsible for this whole racket. I should have put two and two together on that day with that zany panda press tour, when you were speaking badly of her, trying to bring her down a peg because she had wounded your ego. Not a single one of our dumb-faced colleagues said anything bad about her even when they had plenty of opportunities to do so.You were right under my nose the entire time!"

"Wait, this fella works in the publicity department?" Milagros asked timidly. She seemed quizzical about how common and unassuming he looked.

"I sure do! It's the perfect place to use someone's scandals against them if they've wronged you. It was genius really, especially since the new dame on the block was taking all the heat." Cooper smirked and winked at Annabelle. "And unlike you ladies, I have a *real* bean shooter, so no funny games."

Annabelle thought for a split second that he might be bluffing, but there was something about the way he was holding the gun that made her think of all those reckless hotshots back in Texas, toting them around in case some ill-advised duel materialized. It was a real weapon all right, you could tell by the heft of it in his hands. She felt cold sweat form at her hairline, making the wig feel incredibly itchy. She wanted to kick herself for choosing this isolated location as their meeting spot, which could now become their final resting place.

"Well, since you have us at your mercy, and I doubt you'll let us leave unscathed, how about you spill the beans? I think you owe us that," Mae said, hands on hips.

Both Annabelle and Milagros shot her a panicked look. What on earth was this silly Canadian doing? If he wasn't contemplating disposing of them before, he surely was now. Did she manage to read his mind without making that ungodly face or did she have a death wish?

"If I'm quite frank, I didn't start off with a plan," Cooper started, leaning on a tree trunk as if about to embark on a lengthy storytelling journey. "I crossed paths with her on the lot not long after I started working there, and it was love at first sight. But there was always a bunch of fellas hovering around her and I didn't have the courage to speak to her. So, I turned to my trusty pen and paper, pouring out my feelings into letters."

This made Annabelle squirm. Cooper was making it sound like

the beginning of a beautiful love story when in reality it was nothing of the sort. This guy was beyond delusional, and she had to physically stop herself from grimacing in disgust.

"I felt bolder in my letters than I ever did in person, and I was certain that she'd reach out sooner or later. How could she resist such undying devotion?" Cooper continued, in his own little world. "Sure, she went on dates here and there, but I could tell my Clover didn't truly care for those fellas. Then I happened to see her canoodling with that lighting technician and I saw red. Of all people, she would fall for *him*? I was beyond insulted and vowed to get rid of him one way or another. As luck would have it, I found out he was married by snooping through his file in the human resources building and naturally I started blackmailing him. That was an easy first step."

"It sure sounds like that human resources building is easily accessible," Mae mumbled out of the side of her mouth.

Cooper shot her a glare worthy of Gloria Swanson. "As I was saying, I thought making money off this sap would be beneficial until I found the right opportunity to off him. And lo and behold, I found out he'd be working on the set of *The Enchantress*. I was hovering up there in the shadows, waiting for the right moment to strike just as the lights would blind anyone below from seeing clearly above. But then the lights went out on their own, making my job a whole lot easier!"

Annabelle, Mae, and Milagros glanced at one another, the thought of their weird connection with that book having caused an opportune moment for murder sickened them. But who knew such a sicko was on the prowl?

"I was a gentleman and gave her a few days to recuperate." Cooper nodded matter-of-factly, thinking his action was noble. "I was convinced she'd come right to me, sensing I was a shoulder to cry on, but my mailbox remained empty. And that's when I started acting up, thinking of more ways to hurt her. She wouldn't be falling into another man's arm on my watch."

"So that's when you started blackmailing Mrs. Thorne, forcing her to broadcast the affair." Annabelle filled in the blank.

"Bingo!" Cooper snapped his fingers. "You know, our grouchy colleagues are wrong about you. Sometimes you're more than a pair of great legs and a pretty face."

"Well bless your heart." Annabelle's face twitched. She never felt such a strong urge to pounce on someone. Despite her strong emotions, no tell-tale tingly sensation was materializing. She quickly glanced at Milagros, hoping maybe she'd be able to distract this lowlife by conjuring up a tornado, but she only got a small, imperceptible shake of the head as a response. They were really in a pickle.

"I guess this whole thing has turned into a big game of dominoes, everything slowly falling into place," Cooper sighed, pushing himself off the tree as his face turned to stone. "But the thing I hadn't anticipated was for my dear Clover to enlist accomplices to ambush me. That's not very nice, now, is it? I'm terribly disappointed but most of all I'm mad. So how about we use that rope you brought along and practise making knots?"

With the barrel of the gun looming over them, the gals' hands and feet were tightly bound before they were unceremoniously dumped into Clover's luxury car, Annabelle in the passenger seat with Mae and Milagros stuffed in the back like a couple of rag dolls.

"I gotta say it feels nice telling my story out loud. But naturally you'll have to take it to your graves." Cooper leaned into the open window on the driver's side, turned on the ignition, and shifted it into drive. "And I think I'm done sending letters. I owe Miss Halliwell a visit in person. Bon voyage!"

Cooper Mason walked away smugly as the car started moving forward on the slight incline leading toward a perilous drop up ahead. So much for a scenic view.

"That cad!" Milagros blurted, the loudest thing she had ever uttered in their presence. "Leaving us for dead like this."

"Was there possibly a Plan B you hadn't told us about, honey?" Mae asked nervously. "It would be mighty handy right now."

"Hush up, I'm trying to concentrate and save us!" Annabelle blurted, breathing heavy as she closed her eyes, blotting out the frightening view from her mind.

She stopped writhing against the tight ropes bound around her ankles and hands, instead focusing on her growing rage.

How dare this man think he can ruin a woman's life, killing a man in the process, all in the name of love? This need for control and possession of a woman as if she were property was infuriating. And on top of that, she had reached out to another man, her own boss to come in as reinforcement with the coppers to put this matter to bed once and for all. But where were they in her time of need? Nowhere to be found.

"Those useless men, the whole lot of them. I'll give them a piece of my mind!" Annabelle seethed with rage from years of biting her tongue and taking it in stride. Her entire body was being taken over by that unmistakable tingling sensation, the power of it coursing through her as she flung her eyes back open. "Don't worry ladies, it looks like we'll be performing a Houdini escape act today."

Chapter 38

Moments before the car's front wheels would have started their descent over the edge of the cliff, Annabelle concentrated her energy into swerving the vehicle to the left, the force of it momentarily making the back-end teeter over the drop before speeding up and bumping into a tree a safe distance away.

"Jiminy Christmas!" Mae was in awe as she tried to regain a sitting position in the back. "You really waited until the last second to show off, didn't you?"

"Look, he's getting away!" Annabelle snapped her head around and looked out the back window. She could make out Cooper on the trail ahead, his back to the car and completely unaware of her telekinetic stunt.

"We'll see about that," Milagros said before she started muttering Spanish words under her breath.

In utter disbelief, Annabelle and Mae watched as she conjured up the earth, the ground shaking beneath them like an earthquake as a very tall and thick tree uprooted itself, crashing down on the path Cooper was strolling on. A satisfying scream soon followed.

"Quick, quick." Annabelle had managed to break free from her binds and was now helping the others. "We gotta see the damage."

They bolted out of the car and ran halfway up the path, stopping in their tracks when they saw the state of him. Cooper had been pinned on his stomach by the imposing tree, his arms comically stretched out in front of him as a thick web of branches weighed down his back and thighs. It's the flailing feet that got them laughing uproariously.

"What's the meaning of this?" Cooper blubbered as he turned his head and noticed the three of them standing there intact. "How on earth did you get out of the car? It was seconds from tipping over!"

"You're not the only one with a few tricks up their sleeve," Mae smirked. "Looks like you're stuck, huh? Seems to me like you've lost control of the situation, haven't ya?"

Cooper looked absolutely shattered that he didn't get away, he was on the verge of a childish tantrum, and it made Annabelle enjoy this triumph even more .Not only did she manage to save their necks, but she also presumably saved Clover and her unborn child from an equally grizzly encounter.

"What do we do with him now?" Milagros asked, the sun almost officially set. "Should we knock him out and shove him in the trunk?"

"The trunk? You dames wouldn't do that to me, would you?" Cooper laughed nervously.

"Trust me, we want to do much worse to you," Annabelle shot back before turning her attention to her friends. "It's as good a way as any to get him out of here."

195

"There will be no need for that, Miss Stonewood," Mr. Beauregard announced as he made his appearance on the path followed by a handful of police officers. The three friends turned around in surprise, both relieved and peeved at their presence.

"Well, well, well, look what the cat dragged in," Mae scoffed, not hiding her disdain.

"Better late than never!" Mr. Beauregard answered sheepishly, scratching the back of his head.

"Oh yeah? *Late* almost got us thrown down that cliff over there and you would have had three more murders on your conscience. And surprise! The murderer worked under your supervision this entire time." Annabelle moved away so the new arrivals could get a better look at who was being held prisoner by a giant tree.

"*Cooper*? Cooper Mason?" Nelson's eyes nearly bulged out of his head. "You're behind all of this?"

"Hiya, boss. This isn't what it looks like," Cooper replied, his hands groping the ground like a child.

"Is that so? What is it then?" Nelson had regained some of his grouchy composure.

"It's them! They attacked me as I was minding my own business," Cooper blurted.

"Oh yeah? So, they made this tree fall on you?" Mr. Beauregard chuckled as Milagros discreetly winked at her accomplices. "Get him out from under there and search him boys."

As instructed, the coppers pulled him out from his branch prison with much effort and held him firmly as they searched all his pockets. First, they found his gun, then some unsent letters with the exact same handwriting as the killer, followed by a locket with Clover's picture inside.

196

"Gee, do you always walk around with such damning evidence? That's quite embarrassing really," Mae teased, and all Cooper could do was look away. Nothing he could say would make him appear any less guilty.

"What a disappointment." Nelson sighed and shook his head. "Cuff him boys and let's get out of here."

"So long, Cooper. I'm sure you'll have plenty of time to write letters behind bars. Pen pals are quite popular in jail." Annabelle gave him her best pageant smile as her now former colleague was escorted down the path by the coppers.

"Are you ladies all right? I feel downright awful about this. I contacted the police department, and they were very slow at cooperating," Nelson said as he hovered back with the heroines, then grew alarmed when he saw Mae's face. "Are you all right, dear? You do look dreadful!"

"He's lying!" Mae gasped, her face contorting like she ate an entire grapefruit. "He dismissed Annabelle's letter. It's Clover who convinced him this was on the level."

The three ladies glared at him as he was taken aback, the truth slapping him in the face.

"I-I don't understand how you figured it out but sadly yes, it's Miss Halliwell herself who convinced me to come here armed with the city's finest." Nelson grew pale. "I'm very sorry, I should have believed you sooner. I realize that now."

"You're damn right, Mr. Beauregard." Annabelle crossed her arms, nose in the air. "I think from now on you should trust me and give me more publicity responsibilities. One of your employees is going to jail for murder after all so naturally you'll need more of my help."

"Sure, sure anything you say! Let's just please keep this snafu between us?" Nelson pleaded. "I could pull some strings and arrange some bonuses for you lovely ladies?"

"How chivalrous of you," Mae cooed.

Relieved, Nelson escorted them back to Clover's car which was haphazardly parked near the cliff, the doors flung open. He looked around, confused as he noticed rope scattered nearby.

"Gee, so he tied you up, threw you in the car, and put it in drive?" Nelson whistled. "Either you three have a truck load of luck floating around or you're a bunch of escapologists!"

"Something like that," Milagros chimed in innocently.

Chapter 39

"We've been deceived by someone amongst us, someone who's obsession grew deadly," Nelson Beauregard intoned into the microphone as he presided over a well-attended press conference outside MGM's prestigious gates.

Annabelle, Mae, and Milagros hung off to the side, waiting with anticipation to see if the head of publicity was going to go with Annabelle's curated turn of events. She concocted it to minimize questions and steer the conversation in the right direction; she sure hoped her boss followed through. It would be a downright shame if another scandal erupted from this.

"Cooper Mason, one of my newest employees in the publicity department, was lovestruck when he set eyes on Clover Halliwell, our emerging talent. And who could blame him? She is easy on the eyes and talented to boot," Nelson explained, getting a few chuckles from the crowd. At Annabelle's insistence, neither Clover nor Louise were present at this press conference. It would have elicited too much excitement. Instead, they listened from undiscernible parked cars nearby.

"But his infatuation soon grew dark and obsessive, killing Chuck Thorne, the man he thought Miss Halliwell was involved with," Nelson continued, his voice loud and stern to avoid the mere thought of interruptions. "You see, in his twisted mind Cooper created another reality altogether, one where he had the right to manipulate the object of his affection. What's worse, he convinced the poor widow of the man he murdered to come out with this fabricated affair in order to tarnish Miss Halliwell's reputation. Now isn't that downright awful?"

The members of the press reacted sympathetically as the three assistants exchanged a knowing look. The denial of the affair was the best course of action to minimize more snooping into Clover's private life, which would soon be welcoming a new member. A small knot formed in Annabelle's stomach. She didn't enjoy being dishonest, but the press had nothing to gain from knowing this truth. Clover and Louise had buried the hatchet and things could be left at that.

"Now, contrary to popular belief, despite us saying Chuck Thorne's death was accidental, the Los Angeles Police Department and our team smelled a rat. Keeping things as discreet as possible, we worked closely with Miss Halliwell and Mrs. Thorne to nab this culprit who was both a murderer and a blackmailer," Nelson continued, head held high despite this gigantic lie. "We set out a plan to corner this monster once and for all. And in a dramatic showdown by the Hollywoodland sign, we did just that."

"Yeah, you're welcome," Mae muttered from their spot away from the hubbub, arms crossed over her chest.

"I know it's hard to stomach. Trust me, I don't like it either!" Annabelle sighed as she turned to her dejected friends, the three of them being the true heroes in this story. "But the public doesn't need to know all the nitty gritty details. This ensures the studio still looks good despite the fact that the murderer worked under our noses. It might not feel like it, but this is a win for us."

Mae and Milagros replied with noncommittal shrugs as they turned their attention back to Nelson's boastful speech, the press gobbling it up as they scribbled frantically in their notebooks.

"I'm shocked just as you all are, knowing this perpetrator worked under me." Nelson shook his head and Annabelle could sense sincere disappointment and regret behind his words. "I am truly sorry I didn't pay closer attention to what was going on in my department. I had a talk with Mr. Mayer and all the higher-ups here at MGM and we're committed to creating a safe working environment here at the studio."

He took a step back, letting his words sink in before continuing.

"Who knew the behind-the-scenes life at MGM would be filled with as much drama and excitement as any movie we produce?" Nelson chuckled, pivoting rapidly to promotional mode. "And speaking of movies, *The Enchantress* has completed filming and will be making its way to theatres in a few months! You won't want to miss it."

"Well at least he appeared sincere for a portion of that speech." Milagros shrugged.

"That was a miracle I tell ya," Mae shot back. "Fellas like that only have a one-track mind and it's set on making as much kale as possible."

Annabelle looked toward the parked cars around the corner,

and she noticed Louise was trying to get her attention. "I'll be right back, ladies," she said before walking over to her.

"That must have been hard to hear, knowing you helped capture this sicko," Louise said after rolling down her window. Compared to the first time they met, Louise's face was makeup free, and she seemed much more at ease with herself.

"It couldn't have been a walk in the park for you either!" Annabelle offered.

"You know, all of this got me thinking about this perceived idyllic life Chuck and I had created for each other here in Los Angeles. It was all for show!" Louise giggled and sighed. "And now that he's gone, I think the best thing for me is to go back to my family in the Midwest. Things are simple and quiet out there, and I can focus on my happiness without any distractions."

"That sounds swell." Annabelle smiled. "You deserve that peace of mind."

"Thank you for everything you've done." Louise reached a gloved hand out the window and squeezed Annabelle's arm. "These past few weeks have been beyond bizarre but I'm grateful you were in my corner. Take care."

Annabelle waved as Louise's chauffeured car drove off, presumably to the train station. It only had time to turn the corner before she was interrupted from her "simple life" reverie by a loud *"Psst!"* She turned around and noticed a familiar set of white-rimmed sunglasses peeking out from another chauffeured vehicle.

"Were you just chatting with Louise?" Clover asked from her secure, hidden spot in the backseat, only a small sliver of the tinted window was rolled down out of precaution.

"Yes, she'll be all right," Annabelle assured her. "And how about you?"

"Let's just say I'm relieved it's all over. And now that filming is done, I'm Europe bound to deliver this bundle of joy." Annabelle couldn't clearly see through the window, but she knew the rising star was cradling her bump proudly. "I'm eternally grateful you managed to sort out this fiasco and avoid revealing my biggest secret of all. You're a good egg and I'm glad we got to know each other."

"You're going to make me blush." Annabelle waved a hand. "You know, I commend you for seeing this pregnancy through. The men who control the studios and the star contracts don't always have women's best interests at heart, but you wouldn't take any of their bullying. It's inspiring."

"I think the idea of MGM losing me to another studio spooked them enough to let me go on this extended vacation and eventual 'adoption.' But I know what you mean. It's good to know us gals have each other's backs." Clover smiled brightly. "I'll be back soon enough."

Once again, Annabelle stood on the edge of the curb waving at a car driving away. The press conference was officially done, the reporters having dispersed to rush back to their offices to type up their notes. Mae and Milagros came and stood by her, breathing a sigh of relief at seeing this murder investigation finally being put to rest.

Chapter 40

After snacking on some potato chips from the commissary, Annabelle, Mae, and Milagros found themselves walking toward the fake New York City set yet again, the serene atmosphere of the man-made lake calling to them.

"Today should feel like a victory but it all feels pretty lousy to me," Mae said as she chucked a pebble into the lake, making it skip over the top like a frog.

"Yeah, very unsatisfying," Milagros sighed, fiddling with her thick braid.

"It doesn't feel like the eel's hips but trust me it was for the best," Annabelle tried explaining despite also feeling bummed out. "Those vultures from the newspapers are relentless already, can you imagine if they knew the whole truth? Why, they'd be at our heels day and night!"

"If I'm being honest with myself, it's not so much the conclusion of this bonkers murder investigation that has me sore. It's our little dilemma with our new abilities," Mae replied. "It's open-ended and that drives me mad!"

"Pos-i-tutely," Annabelle conceded. "Now that the investigative distraction is out of the way, my thoughts are being consumed by it. How about you, Milagros?"

"Considering the fact that I can turn water into ice and conjure up fireballs, yes it does worry me quite a bit," Milagros answered. "And please call me Mila. We're tied together by this big secret after all, so I think nicknames are a given now."

"Very well, Mila." Annabelle smiled. "You know, despite the predicament we've been forced into, it's nice having each other. Heck, I'm not sure we would have gotten to know each other otherwise!"

They heard the crunching of shoes on earth and turned around in unison to see Velma French standing there timidly with her hands behind her back. Having had some recent frosty encounters with her, none of them were brave enough to speak first.

"It's not true what they said at that press conference, was it?" Velma cleared her throat. "You're the ones who set out to ambush Cooper Mason by the Hollywoodland sign, and you managed to pin him under a tree before the coppers showed up."

"Golly, how did you know?" Annabelle was stunned.

"I ... saw it," Velma mumbled, looking away.

"What do you mean you saw it? Through a crystal ball?" Mae blurted out her zany thoughts.

"No!" Velma's temper briefly flared but she reigned it in quickly as she smoothed out her black bob. "I had a vision as Mr. Beauregard was talking, I saw the whole thing. From the deviation of the automobile away from the cliff to the uprooting of that enormous tree."

"Jeepers, she has the gift of premonitions," Mila exhaled, wide-eyed.

"I take it this isn't the first time you saw the future, or the past?" Annabelle asked, slightly confused about how it all worked.

"As you can probably guess, it all started the day after we came in contact with that prop book." Velma looked around, making sure no other studio employees were lurking nearby. "It was small little snippets at first, like a call Miss Harlow was about to receive, what they'd be serving in the commissary, evening newspaper headlines. It was strange but not too intimidating. Then came the vision of Miss Halliwell receiving those hideous fan letters, which was quickly followed by one of the infidelity headlines. I got the feeling I was supposed to act on these premonitions, and it gave me the heebie-jeebies."

"That's why you weren't in a talking mood when I crossed you in the fan mail department," Annabelle offered.

"You're right on the money and I feel awful about being so rude, but I just didn't know how to react." Velma shrugged. "I wasn't ready to admit this gift was a part of me."

"We've all had our moments, trust me," Mila replied sympathetically.

"Last night I got snippets of your ambush. I saw the three of you hanging around the Hollywoodland sign but there was nothing alarming about it yet. It was only once Mr. Beauregard was blatantly fibbing this morning that I got the full picture. I'm glad you gals made it out all right."

"Well, we can thank their powers for that." Mae pointed toward Annabelle and Mila. "Annabelle has telekinesis, Mila can conjure up the elements, and I am gifted with telepathy. So, it looks like them two have more active powers and we have the more passive ones."

"They're not passive, they've extremely valuable," Mila chided.

"Yeah, yeah," Mae scoffed.

"Anyhoo." Annabelle looked at Mae crossly. They didn't want to spook their new friend into running away. "We're glad you're here now. This is new for all of us and it's important we stick together. It's not every day you get bestowed with new abilities like these!"

"I'll say!" Velma laughed, relieved to be included in this small group of women. "So, what's the plan? I don't know about you gals, but I'd sure like to understand why this happened to us, if we were chosen somehow or if it's a wild fluke."

"There's only one way to find out." Annabelle looked at them intently. "We need to find that darn book."

THE END

About the Author

Dominique Daoust is the author of The Deadly Exclusives Trilogy and The Silver Screen Coven Series. She is a journalism graduate from Concordia University in Montreal, Canada. When not reading or writing, she likes to do yoga, drink margaritas, incessantly quote Friends and listen to rap while doing mundane household chores.

You can connect with me on:
- https://www.dominiquedaoustauthor.com
- https://www.facebook.com/DominiqueDaoustAuthor
- https://www.instagram.com/dominique.daoust
- https://www.tiktok.com/@dominique.daoust.author

Subscribe to my newsletter:
- https://bit.ly/3JWbksN

Also by Dominique Daoust

Dominique Daoust is the author of The Deadly Exclusives Trilogy, a historical cozy mystery series with a dash of supernatural elements. The trilogy is available on Amazon and Kindle Unlimited!

A Disappearance at the Bonne Nuit Hotel
Secret sources have a whole new meaning.

Newbie reporter Rita Larose is tired of getting assigned boring stories at one of Montreal's most popular newspapers. It's 1930 after all, women don't need to only write about household chores anymore! But when a high hat socialite gossips about the New Year's Eve party at the Bonne Nuit Hotel, a riveting mystery falls right into Rita's lap. This is her chance to prove to herself and her underestimating colleagues that she has what it takes to write the hard-hitting articles.

While going undercover as a maid to get the scoop, Rita will soon discover unexpected friendships and an unusual gift of her own to contend with. Will she be able to juggle this newfound ability while not blowing her cover and jeopardizing her career-making article?

Lights Out Revenge

What could possibly go wrong in the dark?

Rita Larose is once again thrown into an investigation after a longstanding member of the Mount Royal Club bites the dust during a parlour game. Not only were the conditions scandalously mysterious, but the nature of this elite, secretive venue makes her all the more curious and hungry for answers.

With the help of her best friend and her hard-headed secret source, they will stop at nothing to grill the dearly departed's temperamental social circle to draw conclusions. What those conversations reveal about her own friendships has her reeling. Will they be able to conquer the absurd amount of lies and deceit before someone else is put in harm's way?

Revelations at the Midnight Circus

The rides aren't the only thing that will have you screaming.

After an unsettling discovery, Rita Larose is looking forward to distracting herself at the Midnight Circus during Halloween season. Spooky performers and thrilling rides, what's not to like? Her fun is short lived when a body is discovered in the haunted corn maze on opening night, leading her once again down an investigative rabbit hole.

If that wasn't enough to contend with, a sneaky rival with ulterior motives is determined to make her life a living hell. These unexpected obstacles force Rita into trying new tactics that lead to upsetting results. With the pressure surrounding her at an all-time high, can Rita race against time to stop this murderer once and for all?